THE REVOLUTION
OF THE MOON

Andrea Camilleri

THE REVOLUTION OF THE MOON

Translated by
Stephen Sartarelli

Europa
editions

Europa Editions
214 West 29th Street
New York, N.Y. 10001
www.europaeditions.com
info@europaeditions.com

Copyright © 2013 by Sellerio Editore, Palermo
First Publication 2017 by Europa Editions

Translation by Stephen Sartarelli
Original title: *La rivoluzione della luna*
Translation copyright © 2017 by Europa Editions

Library of Congress Cataloging in Publication Data is available
ISBN 978-1-60945-391-6

Camilleri, Andrea
The Revolution of the Moon

Book design by Emanuele Ragnisco
www.mekkanografici.com

Cover image: Sir Anthony van Dyck, *A Genoese Noblewoman and Her Son*,
Flemish, 1599 - 1641, c. 1626, oil on canvas, Widener Collection

Prepress by Grafica Punto Print – Rome

Printed in the USA

CONTENTS

To Rosetta

THE REVOLUTION
OF THE MOON

The Viceroy Opens the Session,
but Someone Else Closes It

The session of the Holy Royal Council, held at the palace every Wednesday morning at ten o'clock sharp by the Viceroy, don Angel de Guzmàn, marquis of Castel de Roderigo, began in customary fashion that day, the third of September, sixteen hundred and seventy-seven, in keeping with strictly established procedure.

First on the agenda, five chambermaids opened the windows to let in some fresh air, swept and washed the floor, and dusted and polished the furniture in the great hall.

The six Councillors' armchairs were set up with three on either side of the great golden throne reserved for Their Majesties the Kings of Spain, none of whom had ever, however, had occasion to rest his august buttocks upon it, because none had ever deigned to descend upon the island.

The throne sat at the top of six great stairs covered with a thick red carpet.

To the right of the throne, but a bit forward and lower by three stairs likewise covered in red carpet, stood a smaller throne less gilded than the other. This was where the Viceroy sat. Four steps away from the last of the three armchairs on the left was a large table with two chairs. These were the places of the protonotary and secretary of the Council.

On the wall behind the King's throne hung an enormous, full-figure portrait of His Majesty Carlos, four times life size. Beside the portrait was an enormous wooden crucifix. The sculptor hadn't quite got Jesus's face right, however: instead of showing it twisted up in sorrow and agony, he'd given it an expression of rage and indignation. Knowing such a harsh gaze to be upon them, the Councillors, none of whom had a clean conscience, felt uneasy and would try therefore to avoid looking up at the crucifix.

Once the chambermaids had left, the master blacksmith, Alizio Cannaruto, came in. It was his responsibility to check the iron framework, completely hidden under the gilded wood, that supported the Viceroy's thronelet, which had had to be specially constructed to replace the one used before it.

Once the master blacksmith had left, the master measurer, Gaspano Inzolia, came in with two assistants. The master measurer would check that all the armchairs were perfectly aligned, not one hairbreadth ahead or behind one another. Even the slightest shift of one armchair could upset the Councillors' sensitivities, or be mistaken as a sign of good will or ill will on the part of the Viceroy, or as a sign of arrogance on the part of one member of the Council, and therefore have grave consequences leading to long disputes, squabbles, even murder.

At a quarter past nine, the hall's great gilded double door was solemnly opened by the first ushers of the court, Foti and Miccichè, who then took up position, face to face and stiff as boards, bowing to each Councillor as he entered between them and went to sit down in his appointed place.

They entered with chests thrust out and in formal dress, not bothering to return the ushers' bows, one after the other, in keeping with their rank within the Holy Royal Council: His Excellency Don Rutilio Turro Mendoza, archbishop of Palermo; don Giustino Aliquò, prince of Ficarazzi and Grand Captain of Justice; don Alterio Pignato, duke of Batticani, Chief Treasurer; don Severino Lomascio, marquis of Roccalumera, Judge of the Monarchy; don Arcangelo Laferla, count of Naso, Admiral of the Fleet; and don Cono Giallombardo, baron of Pachino, Grand Master of Administration.

Then the protonotary, don Gerlando Musumarra, came in, followed by the secretary of the Council, don Ernesto Rutè.

At this point the two ushers went to inform the Viceroy's chief chamberlain that all the Councillors were present and standing at attention, waiting for His Excellency, don Angel, behind the closed door, to make his entry.

By now it was half past nine.

When the Viceroy, Marquis don Angel de Guzmàn, first landed at Palermo almost two years earlier, he had surprised everyone for two reasons.

The first was his young age, since he hadn't yet reached thirty, and no Sicilian could remember there ever having been a viceroy less than fifty years old.

The second was his extreme thinness. Don Angel didn't have an ounce of fat on him. His skin clung directly to his bones. He must have weighed, at the very most, barely a hundred pounds. A strong gust of wind would have sent him flying through the air like a dry leaf.

He had come to Palermo alone, but was joined one month later by his wife, donna Eleonora di Mora, who was Spanish but from a Sicilian family and had been orphaned at the age of ten. Upon the death of her parents she'd been shut up in a convent where she was educated, learning Italian, among other things, and did not emerge until she was engaged. Don Angel and Eleonora were newlyweds, in that they'd been married only three months before. Word quickly spread that Donna Eleonora was twenty-five years old and so beautiful it was frightening, though nobody had had any reason to be afraid because nobody had actually been able to see her. Indeed, ever since her arrival, Donna Eleonora had remained holed up in the private section of the palace, in the care of the four chambermaids she had brought with her from Spain.

A month after his wife's arrival, however, don Angel had begun to change radically, before the astonished and increasingly dismayed eyes of the Court.

The phenomenon intially took the form of an extremely rapid fattening of the viceroy's belly, and only his belly, so that don Angel, with the rest of his body still gaunt, looked exactly like a woman nine months pregnant.

But the fatness then quickly spread to his arms, legs and feet. Lastly, it attacked his face. Once a crescent moon, it became a full moon.

In less than six months don Angel weighed over two hundred pounds, and six months after that he was at three hundred. Lately he seemed to have stabilized at four hundred. An elephant.

And there had been no way to arrest the phenomenon. The court physician, don Serafino Gustaloca, during repeated examinations, prodded here and prodded there, gave out medicines galore, administered leeches and enemas, and in the end abandoned hope and threw up his hands. And even a great Spanish doctor, a font of science sent expressly by King Carlos, ended up doing the same.

Even after fasting for a whole week, without drinking so much as a drop of water, the viceroy kept getting bigger and bigger, like a pig being fatted.

The court tailor, Artemio Savatteri, quickly got very rich and had to take on four helpers because he had to remake the Viceroy's wardrobe from scratch every week.

At thirty-five minutes past nine, the door was thrown open, and don Angel's two personal manservants, who had helped him to get dressed, handed the viceroy over to the two ushers. Foti and Miccichè took him by the arms, and don Angel, leaning on them, began to advance towards the Hall of the Council.

Moving was not easy for him. His thighs were so fat that, to take a step, he couldn't put one foot forward as nature decreed, but first had to shift the whole leg to one side and then advance his foot.

But in so doing, his body would lose its center of gravity, totter precariously, and weigh entirely down on the forward leg, and therefore whoever was holding him from that side had to bear the weight of that great mass of flesh. If this person were ever so unfortunate as to lose his balance, he would be squashed at once under the Viceroy's falling body.

As soon as don Angel appeared in the doorway of the hall, the Councillors all rose to their feet, bowed deeply, brought their right hands to their hearts, and waited for the viceroy to settle onto the thronelet before sitting back down.

But don Angel was in the habit of stopping for a moment in the doorway to catch his breath. Amidst the general silence his loud panting sounded very much like a powerful bellows being slowly pumped. Then he resumed his walk, which looked not so much like a walk as the advance of a ship pitching and rolling over rough seas.

The worst, however, was yet to come.

He still had to climb the three stairs up to the thronelet.

Running to take the places of Foti and Miccichè were the protonotary Musumarra and the secretary Rutè, who were the designated assistants to the ushers in such matters.

In front of the first of the three steps, Foti bent down and with both hands grasped don Angel's left foot, raised it with effort, pushed it forward, and set it back down.

In so doing, however, the Viceroy's entire body lurched dangerously backwards and, to prevent his falling, Miccichè had to hold him upright from behind with both arms out-stretched and his own body leaning forward, feet planted tiptoe on the floor, as a counterweight. Finally the protonotary and secretary also had to come up behind don Angel and push until the viceroy had made it onto the first stair.

After granting don Angel the time to work his bellows even harder and rest a little, the operation was repeated in the exact same fashion for the second and third stairs.

Finally, at ten o'clock sharp, the viceroy's four hundred pounds collapsed with a crash onto the thronelet, whose iron frame continued to vibrate for a few minutes after.

The opening of the session was still further delayed a little by the fact that the entire Council remained spellbound by the sight of don Angel's gigantic double-chin, which continued to quiver for a bit like a crème caramel, owing to the vibrations transmitted by the thronelet's iron skeleton.

Once the double-chin's trembling had stopped, don Angel signaled to the protonotary, and don Gerlando Musumarra stood up, declared in the name of the viceroy that the council session was open, and sat back down. The secretary then rose and requested permission to read out the items for discussion on the agenda.

The viceroy turned and looked at the King's empty throne.

He customarily did this before giving an answer of any kind, as if to imply that he was simply the spokesman for the will of His Majesty.

This time, however, he merely sat there staring at the throne and did not answer the secretary—who, immediately convinced that don Angel hadn't heard him, after casting a glance of consultation at the protonotary, repeated the question.

There was no answer. Don Angel sat there without moving, face turned away towards the throne.

He'd been a good viceroy, had don Angel, but over the past month he was no longer really all there. At first he'd shown himself to be an honest man, respectful of the law and his fellow men, ready to condemn injustice and connivance, tyranny and the abuse of power. But then he'd eased up on the reins, and now the councillors did as they pleased.

This was certainly owing to his illness, but also, perhaps, to a rumor that had been circulating for a while among the noblemen of the Council. And the rumor was that the illness had caused every part of don Angel's body to swell to elephantine proportions except one, which was precisely that part that distinguishes a man from a woman, and which, given the new dimensions of the rest of his body, had become practically impossible to locate, more difficicult than a needle in a haystack. Poor donna Eleonora, the gossips said, had become melancholic and fallen mute because of her forced abstinence, and the situation caused don Angel no end of suffering.

Upon the second failure to reply, the Councillors looked at one another in perplexity.

What should they do?

Should the question be repeated a third time? Did they have the right to interrupt the viceroy's silent discussion with His Majesty? No, they didn't. But could they let the entire morning go to waste, staring at the viceroy as he stared at the king's vacant throne?

After five minutes of silence, the prince of Ficarazzi, who in his capacity as Grand Captain of Justice was second in rank only to the Viceroy, stood up and approached the thronelet.

Since he was a lot shorter than the average man yet still much taller than a dwarf, he had to climb all three stairs to come up to the level of don Angel. And at that point he realized that the Viceroy, though indeed facing the thone, had a lost, faraway look in his eyes, which were looking at nothing at all, or perhaps at something so far away as to be equivalent to nothing. The prince of Ficarazzi froze, a bit frightened and not knowing what to do or say.

But the viceroy became aware of his presence. First he gestured as if to shoo away a troublesome fly, but then, ever so slowly, his eyes came to focus on the prince's face. At which point, seeing that the viceroy was looking at him, the Captain of Justice bowed and raced back to his seat.

Don Angel turned his head to look around, as if trying to figure out where he was, as if he'd just woken up from a good long sleep. Seeing the secretary standing before him, he gave him a questioning look.

So the secretary repeated the question a third time.

Don Angel turned his head momentarily towards the throne, and then signaled to him that he was granting his permission. Everyone breathed a sigh of relief. The session was about to open, as every other time.

The secretary stated that the first item for discussion concerned a dispute between the bishop of Catania and the bishop of Messina over the two testaments of the baroness of Forza d'Agrò, in one of which she left everything to the church of Messina, and in the other to the church of Catania. Both bishops had appealed to the Council to adjudicate the matter, and a quick response was urgently needed.

The viceroy looked first at the throne, and then at Archbishop Turro Mendoza, who stood up with a wicked smile on his lips. There wasn't a single person in the hall who didn't already know what the bishop was about to say. They were all familiar with the war that had been raging for years between Turro Mendoza and Gioacchino Ribet, bishop of Catania.

It was a war waged through hearsay, insinuations, gossip, and calumny. Ribet had spread the rumor that Turro Mendoza practiced the foul deed with altar boys, while Turro Mendoza riposted with the accusation that Ribet had impregnated a nun and then had her murdered to avoid scandal.

The bishop of Palermo, who was so short and fat he looked like a ball, had such a loud voice that when he spoke from the pulpit he could be heard as far away as Cefalù. He didn't so much speak words as fire cannons. He said that Gioacchino Ribet was an unscrupulous scoundrel and that the testament bequeathing the inheritance to the church of Catania was clearly forged. He claimed that he had had it carefully examined by experts and had proof to back this up.

The viceroy asked those assembled if they had anything to say about the matter.

Nobody breathed a word. Then don Angel, after looking at the throne, said the question was resolved in favor of the bishop of Messina.

The secretary sat back down and read out the second item for discussion. It was a rather delicate matter. According to a number of anonymous denunciations, barely half of the taxes paid by the citizens of Bivona were reaching state coffers because the other half was being pocketed by the man in charge of collecting them, who was none other than the Marquis Aurelio Spanò di Puntamezza, an extremely rich and powerful man whom one could not afford to offend by casting doubt on his integrity.

As the viceroy was turning around to look at the throne, don Cono Giallombardo, Grand Master of Administration, the man in charge of tax questions, prepared to speak.

And, as had been the case with the bishop, none among those present was in doubt as to what he would say.

It was universally known that Griselia, don Cono's beautiful granddaughter and the apple of his eye, was the mistress of Tancredi Spanò, eldest son of the Marquis of Puntamezza. And everyone knew that the girl's word was law for the Grand Master of Administration. Who, when his turn came to speak, claimed that those anonymous letters were an outrage and not to be taken seriously, as their intention was to blot the reputation of a man known for his rectitude. Indeed the honesty of the Marquis of Puntamezza shouldn't even be up for discussion.

Nobody breathed a word. The viceroy looked at the throne and then declared the matter was unworthy of examination by the Council and should be struck likewise from future matters for consideration.

The third item the secretary came out with was the matter of the *Gloriosa*, the battleship which, upon putting out to sea on its maiden voyage had gone and crashed against some rocks and sunk to the bottom, causing the death of fifteen sailors. The *Gloriosa*'s commander, Captain Aloiso Putifarre, blamed the accident on the fact that the helm did not respond to the helmsman's commands because the ship had been poorly built by the Messina shipyard, which had skimped on the materials used. The master shipbuilder claimed that the fault belonged entirely to Putifarre, who hit the bottle often and hard.

After glancing at the throne, the viceroy gave the floor to the Admiral of the Fleet, don Arcangelo Laferla, Count of Naso.

There was actually no need for the count even to open his mouth, in as much as everyone knew that he was in cahoots with the chief of the Messina shipyard.

Therefore, in the twinkling of an eye, poor Captain Aloisio Putifarre found himself demoted, kicked out of the Navy, and sentenced to prison as the sole party responsible for the accident.

The secretary stood up again, but don Angel signaled to him to approach. The secretary stopped in front of the three stairs. With a gesture of the hand the viceroy invited him to climb the steps, and when the man came up to him, he whispered something in his ear.

The secretary then ran out of the hall. A short while later he returned with Foti following behind him holding a screen under his arm, and Miccichè carrying a urinal covered by a white cloth.

This had happened twice in the preceding month, where

don Angel had an urgent need to relieve himself, but, between stepping down from the thronelet, crossing the hall, reaching his apartment, getting to the privy, urinating, coming back, crossing the hall again and climbing back up the three steps, he made them all lose a good hour at the very least. The solution found by the protonotary and brought discreetly to the viceroy was the best they could come up with.

The two ushers unfolded the screen in front of the thronelet and then disappeared behind it. Amid the silence, all present could hear the powerful, labored breathing of the Viceroy as he stood up, and then the sound of the liquid squirting into the porcelaine vase. It took a good ten minutes. Finally Miccichè reappeared with the chamber pot and left the hall, while Miccichè, after folding the screen back up, followed behind him.

The session could now resume.

But it did not.

Because everyone realized that don Angel was now sitting with his eyes squeezed shut and trembling so violently all over that his wattles were flapping back and forth.

"What the devil is wrong with him now?" the protonotary asked with concern.

"Why is he trembling?" don Alterio asked the bishop.

"Perhaps he's now feeling the need to empty his bowels as well," Turro Mendoza ventured.

Without opening his eyes, the viceroy said:

"*Tengo frio.*"

They all balked. He was cold? On the third of September with a still August-like sun hot enough to split rocks?

The secretary dashed out of the hall, went to speak with Foti and Miccichè, then returned to his place.

Don Cono Giallombardo summoned his courage and leaned down to speak softly with don Arcangelo Laferla. Just to be safe, he put his hand over his mouth.

"Is it not time perhaps to inform His Majesty that our dear viceroy is not in good health?"

Don Arcangelo looked at him doubtfully.

"Are you serious or just joking?"

"I'm serious."

"And so what we need, instead of don Angel, is a viceroy of sound body and mind who can think straight?"

"That's right," said don Cono, ending the discussion.

Two personal manservants came into the hall with a blanket, which they spread over don Angel's legs.

Moments later, the viceroy signaled to the secretary that he could speak now.

Don Ernesto Rutè stood up and began.

"Next on the agenda is a petition from the Prosecutor of Castrogiovanni—"

"Eh?" don Angel interrupted him.

The secretary cleared his throat, coughed a few times, and repeated in a louder voice.

"We're turning to the petition from—"

"Eh?" don Angel said again.

Had he gone deaf?

The secretary took a deep breath, reopened his mouth, and—

"Eh?" don Angel said yet again, before the other had resumed speaking.

At that point everyone realized that this was not a case of deafness. The viceroy was addressing someone whose words he didn't understand and who was surely not in the hall. Don Angel then opened his eyes wide, as if in great surprise, and ever so slowly turned his head towards the throne.

A few minutes went by.

Chapter Two
The Grand Captain of Justice's Brief Day of Glory

The Councillors silently sought each other's counsel, exchanging only quick glances and minimal movements of the head to say yes or no. And they all came to the same conclusion. And thus the Grand Captain of Justice stood up, approached the thronelet, climbed the three stairs, and brought himself up to the viceroy's level. Don Angel sat there motionless, his eyes still goggled wide, and the Grand Captain, with a touch of fright, became immediately convinced that those eyes could no longer see anything. There was a sort of transparent veil over the pupils, a very fine veil, made as if of air but stronger than iron, that henceforth separated the viceroy from the world of the living.

To be certain, the Captain reached out ever so slowly with one hand and with the tip of his forefinger lightly touched—as though afraid to come into contact with his viceroy's flesh— the tip of the viceroy's nose.

There was no reaction.

And so he started to press his finger harder, and little by little, don Angel's head began, under the pressure of his thrust, to fall backwards, like a puppet's.

There was no doubt.

Sitting on the viceroy's thronelet was a corpse.

"I think he's dead," the prince of Ficarazzi, Grand Captain of Justice, said under his breath.

The Councillors all froze, like statues of salt.

The first to rouse himself from the general stupefaction was the protonotary, who stood up and exclaimed:

"We need the court physician at once, to ascertain—"

"Ascertain my ass!" the prince of Ficarazzi retorted, having meanwhile recovered.

This was a situation from which they could all profit immensely.

The protonotary looked at the Grand Captain in shock. Why didn't he want any verification of death to be performed?

"But it would be only right . . . " he insisted.

"And what do we know about don Angel's illness?" the prince cut him short. "Maybe he just looks dead but has only fainted or fallen asleep. If he wakes up and finds a doctor beside him, he might mistake our haste for a desire to see him dead."

"So what should we do, then?" asked the bishop.

This question was exactly what the prince had been waiting for.

"I propose that we carry on with our Council session as though nothing has happened. When we've finished, if don Angel still has shown no signs of life, we'll call the court physician."

"But how will we know whether the viceroy is in agreement with what you put forward?" the protonotary asked doubtfully.

"Silence is consent," said the archbishop, who was a master slyboots and had immediately understood the prince's suggestion.

The protonotary said nothing.

And in the hour and a half that followed, the Councillors took care not only of their own little business matters, but also those of their relatives, friends, and friends of friends. Whole fiefs were transferred from one noble house to another by decree, unsettled inheritances ended up going places where the testators could never have imagined they would go, people with the consciences of wolves were named administrators of Justice and Crown properties, appointed tutors of extremely rich orphan girls, put in charge of miserably failing enterprises. Last on the agenda, a large biannual subsidy, at the request of Simone Trecca, marquis of la Trigonella, was approved for a charitable institution that he had founded the previous year at his own expense.

The protonotary and secretary then stood up, with the former holding the great register of approved measures and the latter holding a quill and ink, and went over to the Grand Captain.

"Your signature," said the protonotary.

"It's not yet time. That would be against the rules and the law," the Grand Captain said, dismissing them.

As the two were heading back to their places, he turned and addressed the Councillors.

"For the time being, I think the fewer people know about the Viceroy's condition, the better. Therefore, let the secretary go and tell the court physician that don Angel has fainted, but without making a big fuss about it. We don't want to arouse people's suspicions."

His tone was peremptory.

It was well known that the law stated in writing that in the case of the sudden death of the viceroy, his position should be temporarily filled by the Grand Captain of Justice, who would remain in power until the arrival of a new viceroy from Spain.

Upon entering, the court physician, having been informed by the secretary that don Angel had lost consciousness, found all the Councillors standing and gathered at the foot of the three stairs, looking quite worried.

"When did this happen?" he asked.

"A minute before the secretary came to get you. We didn't waste any time," said the Grand Captain.

The doctor climbed the three stairs and immediately realized there was nothing more to be done.

He listened to the viceroy's heart, felt for his pulse, brought his ear to his mouth, and then shook his head in sorrow.

"He didn't faint. He's dead," he said to the Councillors. "His heart must have given out, no longer able to support all that fat."

The court physician was quite surprised at the reaction to his words. The Councillors gave themselves over to their grief, making a pitiful scene that touched his heart. The bishop raised his hands to heaven, then fell to his knees in prayer; the prince of Ficarazzi buried his face in his hands; the duke of Batticani started crying without restraint; the marquis of Roccalumera and the count of Naso embraced and consoled each other; while the baron of Pachino, beyond consolation, muttered:

"What a terrible misfortune! What an irreparable loss!"

Then the prince of Ficarazzi, still visibly shaken, said that unfortunately it was the duty of His Excellency the bishop to break the bad news to don Angel's wife and express the profound grief and deepest regret felt by all the Councillors.

Once the bishop had gone out, the prince ordered the secretary to inform the chief guardian that all outsiders present at that moment in the Palace must be thrown out pronto, and told him to send for the Chief of Ceremonies at once.

When the latter arrived, he whispered something in his ear. The Chief of Ceremonies went and looked at the corpse, scratched the back of his head in doubt, came back, and spoke a long time into the Grand Captain's ear. At first the captain shook his head "no," but at the end he threw up his hands and said:

"Well! If there's no other solution . . . "

Fifteen minutes later the Chief of Ceremonies returned, followed by five manservants, all strapping young men, carrying the bier of Santa Rosalia, normally in the chapel, holding it by its long shafts. The Saint's statue had been removed from it and laid on the sacristy floor.

The six manservants set the bier down at the bottom of the three stairs, climbed the steps, lifted don Angel's body with great difficulty, then laid it onto the bier. Then, shouting "Heave!" in chorus, they hoisted the shafts onto their shoulders and exited the hall as everyone present bowed deeply, their heads practically touching the floor.

The court physician asked if he could leave. Before replying, the prince slowly climbed the three stairs and tried to sit down on the thronelet left vacant by the dead viceroy. It turned out, however, to be be too high for him. Planting his hands on the seat, the prince tried to hoist himself up, but was still unable.

At this point the court physician said:

"If Your Excellency will allow me . . . "

As he was a large man, he slipped his hands under the prince's arms, lifted him into the air, and set him down on the thronelet the way one does with a child.

The prince's feet remained in the air, some three palms off the ground. He was swimming inside the thronelet, so much room was there.

"You may go," the Grand Captain said, now that he was seated.

The court physician bowed and went out.

"According to the law, as of this moment I assume the full functions of the office of viceroy. And in keeping with the rule, you must all now pay obeisance to me," the Grand Captain ordered them.

"His excellency the bishop is not present," the protonotary pointed out.

"Let us proceed just the same," the prince replied.

For a moment, nobody budged. Indeed nobody felt like bowing in obeisance to the prince of Ficarazzi, who, though he might well be the Grand Captain of Justice, was still a puffed-up gasbag, according the bishop's definition. But they had no choice. The duke of Batticani rose, stopped at the bottom of the three steps, knelt down, left knee touching the ground, put his right hand over his heart, bowed his head, stood back up and returned to his place. The others did the same.

The prince began to feel like such a giant that he had the impression the thronelet had become too small for him

"Bring me the register, so that I may sign it," he ordered.

His name now carried the same weight as that of the King of Spain.

For a brief moment he felt dizzy.

The assistant Chief of Ceremonies had accompanied Bishop Turro Mendoza into the viceroy's apartment and, after informing Donna Eleonora, had sat him down in an armchair in the antechamber and then left.

The bishop had waited and waited until he forgot he was sitting there waiting and lost himself in thoughts of the choir of altar boys, for whom he had special intentions. At last a door opened and donna Eleonora appeared.

The bishop rose to his feet but had to sit back down at once because he'd gone weak in the knees. Based on the rumors, he'd imagined he would find a beautiful woman before him, but apparently there were limits to his imagination.

The young woman looking at him, waiting for him to speak, was raven-haired, tall, slender, and elegant in her Spanish dress. The finest painter on the face of the earth could never have portrayed her as she really was. And what eyes! Very large and black as ink, they were like a dark and scary night in which one would have been more than happy, however, to lose oneself for all eternity.

The bishop managed to rise, and opened his mouth to

speak, but with a gesture of the hand, with fingers slender, harmonious, and interminable, donna Eleonora stopped him.

"*Ha muerto?*"

How did she know?

The bishop was in any case taken aback by the fact that there was neither anguish nor grief, or anything else, in donna Eleonora's question. It was a simple question and nothing more. As if she had asked about the death of a dog, and not that of her own husband.

"Yes," he replied. "And by the authority of the Council, I—"

Donna Eleonora repeated the same hand gesture.

"*Lo han matado?*" The tone was the same. But what did this woman think the Councillors were? Did she somehow think that don Angel had been slaughtered like a bull in the arena? With everyone looking on? If it had happened in a secluded place, at night, then perhaps . . .

"The viceroy died a natural death. The Lord called him to his side," he replied.

"*Por favor,* I want you to tell the *Gran Capitan de Justicia* that *necesito hablar con él ahora mismo.*"

Then, without another peep or change of expression, donna Eleonora nodded by way of taking leave, turned her back to him, opened the door, and vanished.

The bishop sat there spellbound. What was that woman made of anyway? Stone?

What kind of heart was hiding behind those bottomless black eyes?

All at once it occurred to him that since her arrival, donna Eleonora had not once felt the need to confess. Too bad. Had she taken on a priest as her spiritual guide, he would certainly have known more about this woman who made him so uncomfortable.

"Luckily she won't be staying around much longer," he said to himself, exiting the antechamber.

In the corridor he crossed paths with the bier bearing the viceroy's body on its way to the viceregal apartment.

When he entered the hall of the Council, he saw that they had all left. He was about to turn and leave as well, when he was stopped by a voice.

"Where are you going? I've been waiting for you."

He turned back around. The Grand Captain was still sitting on the thronelet. He wasn't very visible from a distance, rather like a worm on the trunk of an olive tree. The bishop approached.

"You're the only one who hasn't yet bowed in obeisance to me."

The bishop hastily knelt and stood back up.

"Did you inform the widow?"

"Yes."

"Good. The Holy Royal Council will meet again this afternoon at five o'clock. We shall discuss the funeral ceremony, which must be stately and equal to the greatness of don Angel."

"Ah, I almost forgot," said the bishop. "Donna Eleonora wants to speak with you."

"Is she as beautiful as they say?"

The bishop shook his head.

"There are no words to describe her."

"Very well, then, I'll see her after I eat."

"She said she wants to see you at once."

"Oh, all right then," the Grand Captain said with irritation.

The bishop left. If the viceroy had been alive, the captain would have gone at once. Now, however, donna Eleonora had to learn who gave the orders around there.

He remained a while longer in the hall, alone, relishing his little throne.

At half past four Bongiovanni, the master carpenter, went into the hall and replaced the iron-reinforced thronelet that don Angel had used with an older thronelet that he had hastily pounded back into working shape. He'd tilted the seat so that the Grand Captain could remain as though standing, even while appearing to be seated. It would make his diminuitive stature less obvious.

Shortly before the new session was opened, the bishop asked the Grand Captain if he'd spoken with the widow. The prince slapped himself loudly in the forehead.

"I forgot! I'll go after the session of the Council."

He had not forgotten. He'd done it on purpose. It was donna Eleonora who had to be at his disposal, not the other way around.

The session began, with open doors. The Grand Captain had given the order to leave them open so that anyone passing outside the hall could see him seated in all his glory.

One question nagged at him, however. Before speaking, was he or was he not obliged to turn and look at the royal throne, as don Angel used to do? He decided not. Raising his arms to enjoin the councillors to silence, he began to speak.

"We are gathered here for a sorrowful task that we could never have imagined, much less desired. This morning the Lord God recalled to his side the noble soul of don . . . don . . . don . . . "

The ringing stopped and he fell silent, eyes agape and gazing at the back of the hall. Don Cono Giallombardo feared he might be having the same sort of attack as don Angel. All heads turned towards the entrance.

At the edge of the doorway stood a tall, slender woman, all dressed in black, face hidden behind a dense black veil, arms and hands covered in long velvet gloves, also black, naturally. As she began to walk, she looked as if she was floating above the floor, feet not touching the ground.

Amidst the leaden silence, she came forward to the center of the hall and said in a strong, clear voice:

"*Yo soy Eleonora de Guzmán, marquesa de Castel de Roderigo*, and I request *la palabra.*"

An ice-cold shiver, for whatever reason, ran up the Grand Captain's spine like an evil serpent. It cost him great effort to speak, as his jawbones were stuck together and his gullet parched as if he hadn't drunk anything for days.

"Request granted."

"*Con humilidad,* I request of this Holy Royal Council, *y, de manera particular*, of the *Gran Capitan de Justicia*, that my husband's mortal remains not be solemnly buried. *Sólo la bendición para los difuntos*. The bier shall remain *en mi apartamento* till the day of our departure *para España, lo antes posible.*"

The silence grew thicker and weighed down like a boulder on the shoulders of all present.

The Grand Captain's eyes sought out the councillors one by one. But they were all looking at the ground. Ah, so the spineless bastards didn't want to take sides? All right, then, he and only he, don Giustino Aliquò, prince of Ficarazzi, would see to putting the Signora Marquesa de Castel de Roderigo in her place.

"My lady," he said, "I understand perfectly the reasons for your request, but I am sorry to say that I must reject it in the firmest manner possible. The magnificence of the funeral shall let the people see what it means to be Viceroy of Sicily; they shall understand that our beloved King of Spain . . . "

And here he stopped. Because donna Eleonora had turned her back and was on her way out of the hall.

"The session shall resume," the prince said, after a brief pause.

The bishop made a sign that he wished to speak. The prince granted him permission.

"Allow me to point out to you that an agreement could have been reached with donna Eleonora."

The prince turned red with anger.

"Let me remind you that you pledged obeisance to *me*."

"What has that got to do with this? Obeisance is one thing, having a difference of opinion is another."

"So, in short, you do not agree with me?"

"It's not that I do not agree, but if you had simply gone to speak with donna Eleonora this morning when she sent for you—"

"Let it be recorded that Bishop Turro Mendoza does not agree, and then let us proceed. Does anyone have any observations to make?"

Nobody said anything.

At this point the Grand Captain started talking without cease for an hour and a half, discussing down to the finest details the manner in which the solemn funeral should be organized.

First he described how the Cathedral should be decorated and how the chairs should be arranged. Then he explained how the procession, which would start at the palace and end at the Cathedral, should be constituted. At the head, a platoon of soldiers-at-arms, followed by another of sailors, and then the funeral hearse, entirely covered with flowers. Then would come a file of one hundred open carriages bearing the highest authorities in Sicily. The first carriage would have the widow and, naturally, himself, in his capacity as acting viceroy.

The succession of carriages would be determined on the basis of the rank of each authority constituting it. And a great deal of time was wasted working this out. For example: who should come first, the prince of Vicari or the duke of Sommatino? According to heraldic protocol, the prince should come first, but one had to bear in mind that the duke of Sommatino was a dignitary of the Court, while the prince was not.

In short, evening soon fell, and the candelbra were lit.

The secretary's right arm was in spasms from having written so much, while the protonotary got a terrible headache.

But the Grand Captain seemed to have nine lives and kept on fidgeting on his thronelet. The pleasure of power gave him endless energy.

"And now let us determine where the pop . . . the pop . . . "

He wanted to say "populace" but was unable, because through the halflight he'd glimpsed, in the doorway, the tall figure of donna Eleonora.

So she was already back?

And what did the ballbusting woman want this time?

The marquesa, an envelope in her hand, came forward into the middle of the hall, excused herself for the interruption, and asked for permission to speak.

"Oh, all right," the Grand Captain said rudely.

Donna Eleonora said that when looking through the drawers in her husband's desk she'd found a letter addressed to the Holy Royal Council.

"Is it important?" asked the Grand Captain.

"I no open it."

"Secretary, please take the letter from the lady. We'll read it at the end of the session."

"It must be read *con urgencia*," donna Eleonora said firmly.

"I'll decide what's urgent here," said the Grand Captain, face red as a pepper.

"*Es lo que dice* on the envelope," the marquesa retorted.

"Perhaps it's better if we read it," the bishop intervened.

"Let's read it," don Cono Giallombardo and don Severino Lomascio said in unison.

The Grand Captain shot them a withering glance but gave in.

"Very well, then. Secretary, open the letter and read it."

He didn't know that with these words he was consigning himself to his ruin.

The secretary stood up, went and took the envelope, looked at it carefully, and said:

"Indeed it's written on the outside, *To be submitted to the Holy Royal Council and read at once in the event of my sudden death.* There's even don Angel's seal and signature. What should I do, break the seal?"

"Of course," said the Grand Captain.

The secretary broke the seal, opened the envelope, extracted a sheet of paper, and held it up for all to see.

"It is written in the viceroy's hand," he said.

"Go on, go on," the bishop said impatiently.

At last the protonotary began to read aloud.

I hereby express my last will, which I make manifest to all of you in full possession of my faculties and in the exercise of the powers granted to my person by the grace of God and His Majesty King Carlos III of Spain. In the event of my sudden death, my beloved wife, donna Elenora di Mora, marquesa of Castel de Roderigo, is to accede in full to the office of Viceroy of Sicily, with all the honors and burdens, duties and rights associated with said office, while waiting for the Holy Person of His Majesty Carlos III to confirm this, my will, or, failing that, to send another person of his own choosing. For such reason the customary rule that the Grand Captain of Justice should take the office of acting Viceroy in the absence of the latter, is hereby no longer in effect. This is my will, and I wish that it should be accepted and respected by all without delay.

Signed: The Viceroy, don Angel de Guzmàn, marquès de Castel de Roderigo.

The silence was so deep that one could actually hear a fly buzzing around the protonotary's head.

"Holy shit!" were the first words to break it.

It was the bishop who'd said them.

This was followed by a buzz of whispers, muttering, gesticulation and general agitation punctuated here and there with an occasional laugh immediately suppressed.

The prince of Ficarazzi, shaking himself from the tremendous blow that had just stunned him, numbed him, and nearly given him a heart attack, managed with some effort to stand up on the thronelet, as if to tower even more above the others, and shouted:

"This testament is completely worthless!"

"Why?" asked the bishop. "It's written in the viceroy's own hand, and there's even his seal!"

"Because . . . because . . . ," the Grand Captain began, desperately searching for any reason whatsoever for what he'd just said. But not a single one came to mind.

"Let us hear the opinion of the protonotary, who knows the law well," don Cono Giallombardo suggested.

"Hear! Hear!" the other Councillors shouted in chorus, assuming a power of decision they didn't possess.

Don Gerlando Musumarra stood up. Despite the dim light, he was visibly pale and worried.

"There is little to say. The law speaks clearly on this and leaves no room for doubt. The will of the viceroy is supreme and incontestable, whether it is expressed vocally in the presence of witnesses or in written form. As in this case. And it must be applied, even if the entire Council is against it."

"But it's the will of a dead man!" the Grand Captain cried.

"Aside from the fact that this should grant it greater weight, this will of don Angel's was declared, in writing, when he was still alive," the protonotary replied coldly.

The Grand Captain, though he felt in his gut that the entire Council was against him, wouldn't give up the bone.

"But the rule can't be changed by the viceroy; it can only be changed by the King himself!"

"But the rule has not, in fact, been changed," the protonotary replied. "Indeed the deliberations conducted today have been signed by you, my prince, subsequent to the viceroy's death. Therefore, after his death, the viceroy has continued, through your agency, to manifest his will. If we call into question his testament, we must of necessity also call into question all the deliberations conducted by the Council this morning, since they do not bear don Angel's signature."

This was a low blow on the part of the protonotary. It implied that all the misdeeds, favors, abuses of power, and outrages that the Councillors had enacted into law while pretending that the viceroy had merely fainted and not died, risked never seeing the light of day.

The prince of Ficarazzi remained silent for a moment. And the bishop took advantage.

"Why don't we put the approval of the testament up for a vote?" he asked, his face an expression of cherubic innocence.

The Councillors took to this like fish to water.

"Vote! Vote!" they said in chorus.

The Grand Captain realized he'd lost. He sat back down on the thronelet.

"Do as you wish."

"Whosoever considers the testament valid, raise his hand," said the protonotary.

Five hands went up. Don Angel's testament had been approved.

They all then turned around to look at donna Eleonora, who had remained immobile and silent all the while in the middle of the hall.

"You're in my place," she said to the prince, though there was nothing imperious in her tone.

But the prince took fright at the very lack of arrogance in her voice. The woman's coldness made his blood freeze. Bowing his head, he descended from the thronelet and returned to his place as Grand Captain.

Donna Eleonora crossed the great hall before the spellbound eyes of all present, stopped in front of the empty throne of the king, bowed her head, stepped aside, gracefully ascended the three steps, sat down on the thronelet, adjusted her dress, then slowly raised the black veil, uncovering her face.

It was as though there had suddenly appeared, in the darkness of the hall, a point of light brighter than the sun so dazzling that it brought tears to one's eyes.

"You must all give me *el signo de vuestra obediencia*."

This time, too, there was nothing peremptory in her voice. It was only a simple, polite request from a lady of the high nobility.

The Councillors, no longer giving a damn about hierarchy, all shot straight to their feet, including the Grand Captain, who was likewise spellbound, and raced towards the thronelet, shoving and elbowing one another, congregating at the bottom of the three stairs and then kneeling, hands over their hearts and heads bowed.

At that moment don Cono Giallombardo couldn't refrain from whispering:

"So lovely!"

"So lovely!" said the other five Councillors.

"Really really lovely!"

"Really really lovely!" the others repeated.

"A heavenly woman!" said don Cono.

"A heavenly woman!" chanted the others.

Donna Eleonora interrupted the adoration.

"Go back to your places."

They walked away regretfully, heads still turned towards her, like someone having to leave a fresh spring while still thirsty.

Donna Eleonora spoke.

"I confirm that *no habrà* any solemn funeral *y ninguna visita de condolencias*. El Holy Royal Council will meet again the day after tomorrow *a la misma hora que hoy. La sesión ha terminado*."

How was it that, in the twinkling of an eye, while the Council was still in session, all of Palermo found out that the viceroy, who'd died that morning, had been replaced by a woman? Most people didn't believe it, and concluded that it was a joke. It was inconceivable that a woman could be in a position to govern Sicily.

You couldn't really say they were wrong, once you considered how things had gone in recent times.

In sixteen hundred and eleven, one week after landing in Palermo, the Viceroy of Sicily, the Duke of Osuna, had written to the king, in these exact words: "No one here is safe, not even in his own house. This Kingdom recognizes neither God nor Your Majesty; all is for sale, including the lives and possessions of the poor, the properties of the King, even Justice itself. I have never seen or heard of anything comparable to the criminality and disorder here."

And since he was a man with cojones, he sought to make law and order prevail again. And he succeeded, in part, using an iron fist. But then he had to return to Spain, and the situation got worse than before.

Taxes, duties, levies increased by the day, without any apparent reason, and they were applied to everything: wheat, flour, chickpeas, fava beans, silk, cloth, eggs, cheese . . . All that was missing was a tax on the air, just to complete things.

And, as if this weren't enough, the plague and cholera also played their part, having taken a shine to the city, and every so often they would drop in to say hello, leaving behind a trail of corpses and starvelings who could no longer scrape by.

Then even the animals on the farms began to die of hunger, because the peasants no longer had any money to buy fodder. The viceroys had no idea how to deal with the gravity of the situation. As if this weren't enough, a great famine broke out.

In 1647, drought and the frightful increases in taxes finally triggered the bloody Palermo uprising.

There were hundreds of deaths, as well as looting, fires, whole families slaughtered. The people's rage against the merchants, the rich, and the nobility knew no bounds. Spanish soldiers were drawn and quartered in their barracks.

Then, by the grace of God, little by little the carnage ceased. But the consequences lasted a long time, in the form of orphaned boys and girls of all ages who had nothing to eat and resorted to stealing and alms-begging; widows and girls who had nothing to sell but their bodies; and continuous acts of violence and rampant corruption common to all.

These consequences were still present, and perhaps even aggravated, at the moment of don Angel's death. Therefore, if a man hadn't been able to resolve them, certainly a woman couldn't either.

Since, in fact, it was well-known that a woman was worth far less than a man. And sometimes even less than a good animal.

And if, by chance, she should get it into her head that she was worth more, she must be put back in her place at once. And indeed . . .

Palminteri the tailor dashed home and, the minute he entered, started thrashing his wife.

"Wha'd I do? Wha'd I do?" the woman asked, crying.

"Nothing. I just wanted to remind you who gives the orders around here!"

Michiluzzo Digiovanni, a twenty-five-year-old strong as a bull, likewise went home, stripped his wife, laid her down on the bed and got down to work on her for three hours straight, as if she was an animal. And when his wife begged him to stop because she felt her spine cracking and asked him why he was doing this, Michiluzzo replied that he was getting his revenge.

Young Baron Tricase determined that henceforth his wife would never eat with him again and would have to do so alone and serve herself in a little room next to the kitchen where the servants normally ate.

Don Pasquali Pisciotta, a textile merchant, told his wife that from now on, whenever she asked him for food money, she would have to kneel.

And so, when the Councillors went down into the great courtyard to get into their carriages, they found themselves assailed by a great many friends and acquaintances who were dying of curiosity.

"How did it happen?"

"What's going on?"

"How is it possible that a woman . . . "

"This is worse than a revolution!"

Don Alterio Pignato had just managed to climb into his carriage when a man, stepping onto the footboard and hoisting himself up, appeared in the window. It was the Marquis della Trigonella, don Simone Trecca.

"Forgive me, don Alterio, for taking your time, but I wanted to know whether the petition for assistance for my charitable institution— "

"I'm happy to say that the proposal we'd agreed upon was approved this morning without any difficulties."

"I thank you from the bottom of my heart. I never doubted your generosity. And if you'd like to do me the honor of visiting my charitable institution, the doors are always open for you. You know the address."

Don Alterio thought about this for a moment.

"I could drop in tomorrow, an hour after sunset."

"I'll be waiting for you."

At the first light of dawn the following day, anyone passing outside the two palazzi giving onto the Cassaro realized that, on the façade of one, somebody had hung, anonymously and during the night, a scroll with the words:

A woman as viceroy is something to dread,
we all know that women are good only in bed.

While on the façade of the other hung a second scroll with a completely different message:

The men of the Council are so rotten and cruel,
They deserve to submit to a woman's rule.

The city had expressed its opinion. But since the opinions were two in number, and completely opposed, they ended up, as was always the case in Sicily, being of no consequence whatsoever.

* * *

The best coffinmaker in town, 'Ngilino Scimè, had been rather quick in preparing a giant casket for don Angel. He'd simply adjusted to the late viceroy's measurements a coffin he'd set aside for the baron of Ribolla, a man of great size who'd been at death's door for six months but couldn't quite take that final step.

With the help of two coffin-bearers, he brought the casket to the Palace at nine o'clock in the morning.

And so the body, having been blessed the previous day by Don Asciolla, the priest of the palace chapel, was boxed, taken into a small room prepared for that purpose, and set down on an iron stand.

Donna Eleonora had four huge candlesticks placed along the sides, ordering that the candles must remain always lit, night and day.

Then, for the first time since her husband's death, she fainted. She'd spent the night keeping vigil over don Angel's body.

Concerned, the chief chambermaid ran to the Chief of Ceremonies, who raced off to get the court physician, don Serafino Gustaloca.

Who, never having had occasion to see donna Eleonora before, not only nearly fainted himself at the sight of her, but also realized immediately that he'd fallen hopelessly in love with the woman.

Don Serafino was a big man of about forty-five, pale and unkempt, who for his entire life had done nothing but study medicine. He was a sincere, honest man with many good qualities. Having never married, he lived with his mother and an older sister, who was also unattached.

This was the first time he'd felt love for anyone, and since he had no experience, he didn't know how to hide it, no matter how much he would have liked to. And so he let it show at once, remaining spellbound as he gazed at donna Eleonora.

He immediately forgot who he was, where he was, and what he was doing there.

Luckily, since all strength had deserted him, his bag of herbs and medicines fell from his hands, and the thud it made upon hitting the ground roused him from his reverie.

He immediately wanted donna Eleonora's chambermaids to undress her and put her to bed, while he waited in the next room. Then he went in, all sweaty and with throat parched, held out a trembling hand, and touched donna Eleonora's forehead as she stared at him.

Then he took one of her hands to check her pulse and, for a brief moment, got the impression that the lady's fingers had squeezed his own. He was overcome by dizziness and fell into a chair that luckily happened to be nearby.

Donna Eleonora smiled to herself. She'd made a friend, and she realized she needed friends.

The court physician, stammering a little, explained to the chief chambermaid how to prepare an infusion with an herb he kept in a little sack, and he told donna Eleonora that he would wait in the next room. But the lady asked him to stay and sit down.

With heart beating madly, don Serafino obeyed.

Donna Eleonora then asked him whether don Angel had suffered. Don Serafino ruled that out categorically.

Donna Eleonora closed her eyes for a moment, then re-opened them and asked a second question. Who had gone to get him?

The secretary.

And what exactly had he said to him?

That the viceroy had simply fainted.

Donna Eleonora then asked him another question that even someone so naive as don Serafino realized how cunning it was. In his opinion, for how long had the viceroy been dead when he declared him so? Don Serafino was immediately convinced he could only tell her the truth. He replied that the Grand Captain had told him that they'd sent for him at once, but that in his opinion, as an experienced physician, don Angel had died at least two hours earlier.

"Ah!" said donna Eleonora.

The herbal tea arrived. Don Serafino wanted to administer

it to her himself, but when he slipped one hand behind her neck to support her head, he began trembling so violently that he very nearly spilled the cup onto the bed. The chief chambermaid intervened as the doctor was collapsing in his chair, exhausted.

A short while later, donna Eleonora's eyelids began to droop.

"*Tengo sueño.*"

Don Serafino stood up.

"*Por favor*, come back this afternoon."

Don Serafino felt as if he'd shot through the ceiling and was flying through the sky.

"As you wish, my lady."

"*Necesito hablar de nuevo con Usted.* But don't leave through the main door. There is a secret exit Estrella will show you. Use that one. I use it *almost todos los días.*"

"You?" don Serafino asked in surprise.

Donna Eleonora smiled slyly.

"*Yo conozco Palermo mejor que Usted.*"

"But how were you able to go unrecognized?"

Donna Eleonora's smile became slyer than ever.

"I know how to be careful."

* * *

"Serafi, what's wrong? Tell your mama. Why aren't you eating?" asked donna Sidora, the court physician's mother.

"Do you feel sick, Serafi?" asked Concittina, the doctor's sister.

But how could don Serafino have any appetite with donna Eleonora always in the forefront of his mind as though she were present in the flesh?

On top of this, upon returning home he'd been immediately set upon by the two women, who wanted to know whether the viceroy's widow was as beautiful as everyone said, how she was dressed, how she carried herself . . . It was sheer torture.

He withdrew to his room, but couldn't stand it. Though it was full of the books he loved so much, it looked as squalid as a cave now.

And so he locked himself in the privy, took off all his clothes and washed himself all over, to cool himself off. He was burning up, as if from a high fever.

He changed clothes and went outside for a long walk. Two or three times he very nearly got squashed by a passing carriage. He wasn't all there. At five he was outside the palace.

He knocked on the small door in back, as Estrella, the chief chambermaid, had shown him, and a guard opened it. Estrella was waiting for him in the antechamber. The court physician asked her whether the marquesa had eaten. She had. A light broth and a little salad, after which she'd gone back to bed.

When he entered the bedroom, he found donna Eleonora asleep. He sat down without making the slightest sound and stayed here, spellbound, gazing at her.

All at once he noticed two big tears roll out of her eyes. He dried them for her.

A short while later the marquesa re-opened her eyes, saw him, and smiled.

Don Serafino noticed something strange. It was as though the bells of the cathedral had started ringing joyously in his head. He and the marquesa spoke for a long time, and then she told him she had to get up and dressed, because she was expecting some people.

By the time he left, an hour after sunset, he'd answered a good hundred questions put to him by donna Eleonora.

On his way home, for the first time in his life, he started singing. But softly.

CHAPTER FOUR
*Donna Eleonora Presides over the Holy Royal Council
to Everyone's Displeasure*

A nd as don Serafino was returning home happy as a lark, an anonymous carriage, with no coat-of-arms, pulled up outside a small palazzo, freshly painted and three stories high, which stood a bit out of the way, along a secluded and poorly maintained road.

The coachman, who'd been instructed not to wear his livery, hopped nimbly down from his seat and went to open the door.

The duke of Batticani, don Alterio Pignato, got out, looking carefully around. He kept a handkerchief over his face as though he had a cold.

"Should I wait for you, sir?" the coachman asked.

The duke hesitated a moment, as though doubtful.

"No, this may take a while. Let's do this: come back to get me in two hours, and if I'm not done yet, wait for me."

After the carriage had gone, he knocked on the door, putting the handkerchief back over his face. The little door inside the big door was immediately opened by don Simone Trecca himself.

"I heard you arrive and rushed to come and greet you."

"My dear marquis, as you can see, I have kept my word."

"And here I am, my lord duke, ready to welcome you with all the honors you deserve."

He stepped aside and don Alterio came in. Don Simone closed the door. All the candelabra were lit.

"On the ground floor," don Simone explained, "are the

chapel, the refectory, the kitchen, two small water closets, an office, and the great room in which the poor orphan girls learn the art of sewing. Would you like to visit the rooms?"

Don Alterio didn't feel like it and pretended he hadn't heard.

"How old are they?"

"Between sixteen and twenty. They're all girls from good families, daughters of tradesmen, clerks, tailors, and barbers, who've had the bad luck to lose their parents and means of support."

"How many have you got here at the moment?"

"Right now there are scarcely twenty-five, but with the generous donation you were so good as to win me from the Council, I should be able to house about forty."

So saying, he licked his lips.

"And where do they sleep?"

"There are twenty on the first floor, and five on the second, which is mostly empty. But the cells for new arrivals are ready."

"And who's on the top floor?"

"The two watchwomen, four chambermaids, and the master seamstress. And then there are the storerooms in which all the things necessary to the maintenance of the house and the girls are kept."

"Why is it so quiet?"

Don Simone smiled.

"According to house rules, the girls eat at sunset, and afterwards they go into the chapel to pray, and then straight to bed. Wake-up time is four o'clock in the morning. After prayer, they all get down to work. Would you like to go upstairs?"

Don Alterio felt a little disappointed. According to the rumors he'd been hearing from various quarters, this was not how it was supposed to be.

"Well, if they're already asleep . . . "

"It's still worth a visit, believe me."

Don Alterio climbed the stairs behind don Simone.

He found himself in a dimly lit corridor that looked exactly like a convent. There were twenty-two doors, eleven on each side. At the far end was another staircase, leading to the floor above.

"Would you like to look inside the cells?"

"But you would have to open the doors . . . "

"Every door has a spy-hole, and the girls are required to keep a candle always lit inside their cells. Have a look: it's quite a sight."

Don Alterio brought his eye up to the spy-hole of the first door. The candle produced sufficient light.

It was a spartan cell, with a cot, a nightstand, a prie-dieu, a basin on a stand, a jug with water for washing oneself, a bucket for dirty water, a chair, and a clothing rack on the wall.

A girl of about eighteen was sleeping on top of her sheets, given the intense heat. Her nightgown was hiked up to just below her belly, revealing a pair of thighs that made one immediately want to stroke them.

Next don Alterio thrilled at the sight of a twenty-year-old bottom, a pair of white tits as solid as marble, and a Mons Veneris whose thicket looked like velvet . . .

He would have kept on peering into all twenty cells, and even into the privies, had don Simone not said:

"Let's go upstairs."

Climbing the stairs, he turned round to announce:

"Now you'll meet the five most beautiful ones."

Here the cells were each illuminated by three candles. Inside the first was a slightly plump blonde, followed by three vacant cells, and in the fifth was a redhead whose flesh seemed made of iron ore. After three more vacant cells, there was . . . a miracle of God.

Don Alterio stared at her, spellbound.

She was about eighteen, tall, with long black hair falling

over her shoulders, interminable legs, and standing in the middle of the room with her thighs spread. Realizing that there was someone outside looking at her, she slowly raised her nightgown, stripping naked and then running her hands over her hips. In defiance.

"Would you like to see the last two?"

"No."

"Do you like this one?"

"Yes."

"She's one of the ones you can ask to do anything. She makes no fuss and never says no."

"So much the better. Am I supposed to pay her?"

Don Simone seemed shocked.

"But what are you thinking? Are you joking? What do take her for, a whore? She's a poor orphan girl, the daughter of a major-domo of the prince of Lampedusa. Her name is Cilistina Anzillotta. I had her taken in here after she was brought to my attention by the baron—"

"Fine, fine," don Alterio cut him off.

"Well, here's the key to her door. But be sure that when you've finished, you lock her back in. That girl's a devil, she's liable to run away. I'm going to go and spend a little time with the blonde. When you're done, take a peek into the spy-hole. If I'm still inside, knock and I'll come out. If I'm not there, I'll be waiting for you downstairs."

Two hours later, don Alterio came out of the cell, locking the door behind him. He was short of breath. The girl had worn him out. Don Simone was not in the blonde's cell. Don Alterio found him waiting for him downstairs.

"All's well?"

"All's well."

"Do you need anything else?"

"No, thanks. But I wanted to ask you something."

"Speak."

"Could I come back the day after tomorrow?"

He would have gladly spent the whole night with Cilistina. She'd gotten under his skin. But he absolutely couldn't. His wife Matilde was waiting for him at home and would raise the roof if he didn't return.

"My dear duke, you are free to do as you please here. I will remind you only that the sooner I receive the donation, the better it is for everyone."

During the same hours in which don Alterio Pignato, to his great satisfaction, was visiting don Simone Trecca's charitable institution, five Councillors were meeting at the home of the prince of Ficarazzi, the Grand Captain of Justice.

Unexpectedly summoned by the prince, they'd come in secret, without being noticed, on foot, their hats pulled down over their eyes and their cloak collars raised up over their mouths.

The only one missing was don Alterio, whom nobody could find.

"I'll get straight to the point, so as not to take up your time," said the prince. "I've summoned you here because last night I spent a long time thinking about what happened yesterday at the Holy Royal Council, and I've come to a few conclusions."

Everyone immediately thought that the prince wanted to rehash the question of don Angel's testament. But since there was nothing more to be done at this point . . .

"You must realize, prince," the bishop began, "that the late viceroy, in expressing his will that—"

"That's not what I wanted to discuss. For me, it's water under the bridge," the Grand Captain interrupted him.

"Then what are you referring to?" asked don Severino Lomascio.

"The drunkenness," said the prince.

The Councillors looked at one another in bewilderment.

"What drunkenness? Nobody was drunk," said don Arcangelo Laferla, confused.

"We were all drunk! All of us!" the prince retorted, raising his voice and getting all worked up. "We were drunk on donna Eleonora's extraordinary beauty and didn't know if we were coming or going! We practically put her on the altar and made her a saint!"

"That's true," said don Cono Giallombardo. "But it was a spontaneous gesture, an homage, and—"

"And if we're not careful, it could cost us all very dearly," the prince concluded.

"In what sense?" the bishop asked cautiously, as he was thinking in dismay that the Grand Captain was showing himself to be less a fart of hot air than he'd previously thought.

"In the sense that this woman, in the twinkling of an eye, could, if she wanted, reduce us to a bunch of puppets in her hands."

"Indeed . . . " the bishop admitted, after a moment of thoughtful silence.

"But what can we do to protect ourselves?" don Cono asked. "It is so enthralling to gaze at beauty! We can't very well sit around at Council with our eyes closed!"

The prince resumed speaking.

"I'll try to explain. Since I consider donna Eleonora a dangerous woman who has a very clear sense of what she wants to do, and since I do not think that what she wants to do is the same as what we want to do, I say that the first thing we must turn our thoughts to is how we might keep, under her rule, the same freedom of movement we seized when don Angel fell ill."

"But how will we ever say no to what she wants? Her will is law," said don Severino Lomascio who, as Judge of the Monarchy, knew about such things.

"It'll take time, but we'll manage. Meanwhile, the six of us must always be of the same mind in her presence," said the prince. "I propose the following. Every Tuesday—in other words, the day before the Council—we must meet and discuss the matters to be deliberated the following day, and then show up at the Council already in agreement. And we must not budge one inch from our agreed positions. Which means that it may happen that a law will be passed only at the behest of donna Eleonora, and against the opinion of the entire Council."

"And what do we get out of that?" asked don Cono. "The law will pass just the same."

"But haven't you noticed that the city is split in two between those who are for and those against having a woman as viceroy? We must take advantage of this situation. We must make it known to those against a woman viceroy that we Councillors are not in agreement with her. We need to get the entire population on our side."

"That won't be easy," said don Cono.

"Why?"

"Because, based on the impression I've been getting, the women of Palermo are dancing for joy at the idea that the person giving the orders is a woman."

"Not my wife," said don Arcangelo. "When she found out how beautiful donna Eleonora is, she got jealous and made a scene."

"So did mine," said don Severino Lomascio.

The prince called them to order.

"We're talking about serious matters here, if you please. And so, given the situation, we shall propose that all our sessions must be open to the public."

"And then what?"

"And then, after a fire here, a little insurrection there, and a few deaths thrown in for good measure, we can write a nice letter to His Majesty in Spain in which we'll say that the situation here has become serious, and that donna Eleonora, through her stubbornness, is pushing it over the edge. What do you think?"

"That makes sense to me," said the bishop.

The others were of the same opinion.

"In the meantime, however, careful," the prince resumed. "Donna Eleonora must be treated as she deserves."

"And how is that?" asked don Cono.

"With respect, devotion, and admiration. She must have the impression that we are always kneeling before her. I've given instructions to the Chief of Ceremonies that at every meeting, starting tomorrow, there must be six large bouquets of flowers at the foot of the thronelet, one for each Councillor."

"And who's going to pay for them?" asked don Severino Lomascio, who was a bit of a tightwad.

"We'll all take turns. By spending ten, we might earn a thousand," said the prince.

Half an hour later, the meeting ended.

Though the Councillors didn't notice anything, the moment they entered the great hall and sat down at their places, congratulating themselves on the wonderful flowers at the bottom of the three stairs, the palace was completely surrounded by armed Spanish soldiers, under a captain's command. And nobody was allowed to enter.

Then donna Eleonora appeared, and all present rose to their feet. She crossed the room as though flying a span above the ground, then stopped when she saw the flowers. She turned to look at the Councillors and smiled.

The six Councillors all began to sway like treetops in the wind.

"If she keeps smiling like that, we're screwed," don Cono thought.

"*Muchas gracias*," said donna Eleonora.

What a voice! Heavenly music! A melody of angels!

Donna Eleonora went and sat down on the thronelet, the seat of which had been made perfectly horizontal again.

But before the protonotary asked permission to declare the session open, a strange thing happened.

A sharp noise, like a shot from a rifle, came from the door. Everyone turned around. It had been made by the clicking heels of General Miguel Blasco de Timpa, commander of the Spanish forces in Sicily.

The general stood stock-still, in military salute, staring at the thronelet with the frightening eyes of a warrior unaccustomed to showing pity or consideration for anyone.

Donna Eleonora gestured to him to advance.

The general came forward with a martial step, his cavalry sabre and decorations tinkling, and stopped at the foot of the three stairs, though slightly to one side.

He planted himself there like a pole, legs spread and arms crossed.

The Councillors looked at one another, a bit worried.

What was going on? Never before had the commander of the army taken part in a Holy Royal Council. It wasn't his place. So what could it mean?

Donna Eleonora gave no explanation.

Instead, without a word she pointed her index finger at the protonotary, who declared the session open. The secretary rose at once, but donna Eleonora raised a hand to stop him, saying that before anything else, she wanted to made a *declaración de apertura*.

Speaking slowly, to avoid all misunderstanding, she asserted that she had good reason to believe that during the last Holy Royal Council, her late husband, for all practical purposes, had not been in any condition to understand what was happening around him.

She pointed out that that same morning, after he'd woken

up, don Angel had fainted twice, and his two personal manservants could attest to this.

She added that she'd begged him to postpone the Council, but he wouldn't hear of it.

For this reason she maintained that it was her duty to have all the measures taken at the last Council annulled, and that they should all be discussed anew in the present, just-opened session.

The first to realize what donna Eleonora's words meant were the bishop, don Cono, and don Severino.

They shot to their feet and started yelling like madmen, saying that the measures taken had been approved by the viceroy and could not be reversed.

"What's done is done!" the bishop blurted out.

"We are men of our word!" don Severino said, indignant.

"There is no turning back!" don Cono fretted.

The other Councillors, who finally understood, also rose to their feet and started raising hell. Then, without even realizing it, all six started moving towards the thronelet. Of course they had no intention of laying their hands on donna Eleonora; they simply did it instinctively, perhaps to make themselves better heard.

At this moment General Miguel Blasco de Timpa sprang into action. With two powerful kicks he sent the bouquets of flowers flying, giving himself more room to maneuver, and as his right hand was reaching for the hilt of his sabre, he stuck two fingers of his left hand in his mouth and let out a shepherd's whistle that shattered the Councillors' eardrums. At once twelve armed solders appeared and quickly placed themselves between the general and the Councillors.

The latter, arms raised in terror as if to surrender, immediately ran back to their places without another word.

Upon the general's order, the soldiers went and took up position behind the king's empty throne. At this point the secretary, trembling like a leaf, asked for permission to speak. When granted it, he said that a number of the measures taken had already been communicated, upon his instruction, to the people concerned, because he'd considered them valid. So how should he now proceed?

Donna Eleonora, after thinking about this for a moment, said that the notifications, in her opinion, should be respected. Were the Councillors in agreement?

"Aye," the Councillors said in chorus.

Therefore all that had to be reviewed, and reopened for discussion, were the measures not yet made public. Which were these?

It turned out they were all those that had been taken after don Angel had died and everyone had pretended he hadn't.

The deliberations lasted three straight hours.

All the measures that donna Eleonora opposed, the entire Council approved. What the prince of Ficarazzi had predicted was happening.

However, since the will of donna Eleonora was sovereign, all the measures were annulled.

At this point donna Eleonora proposed that the session be continued the following day.

The bishop took exception to this, claiming that while he indeed had precise obligations to the Crown, he had higher ones to God and the Church, and the following morning he would be engaged in a service at the Cathedral.

Since they had all decided the previous day that should make a show of unanimity at the Council, the prince of Ficarazzi decided this was a good moment to declare that he, likewise, could not be present at such a session, in as much he already had an engagement in Catania for that day. And quickly, with one excuse or another, the remaining Councillors all stated that it would be impossible to hold any sort of meeting the following day. And so donna Eleonora asked them how many days they could devote to the Council, aside from Wednesday. In the name of all the Councillors, the prince of Ficarazzi replied that Wednesday was the only day available.

Donna Eleonora replied that this was not enough; there were too many other things to be done.

The prince of Ficarazzi threw up his hands. Deep down he was relishing the difficulty he was creating for her.

Donna Eleonora beseeched them to seriously reconsider their position. Could they find at least three days to devote to the Council?

"No," said the prince.

"*Ni siquiera dos?*" asked donna Eleonora.

"No," said the prince.

Donna Eleonora turned to the secretary and ordered him to put on the record that none of the Councillors had been willing to put himself entirely at the disposal of the Viceroy.

Then she said:

"*La sesión ha terminado.*"

She rose and exited in haste, followed by the general and the soldiers. The Councillors sat there for a moment, perplexed. Then the prince went over to the protonotary, followed by the other Councillors.

"Why did she have you enter into the record that we were not entirely at her disposal?" he asked.

"Because in so doing, if you'll forgive the expression, she stuck it straight up your asses," was the unexpected reply.

The Councillors were dumbstruck.

CHAPTER FIVE
It's War between Donna Eleonora and the Councillors

"W
hy?" the Grand Captain asked as soon as he'd recovered, drenched in a cold sweat.

"Why?" the others all asked in unison.

Seeing all those anxious faces, don Gerlando Musumarra, the protonotary, was tickled pink.

"Because, my illustrious lords, the law speaks clearly. Had you known it, you wouldn't have got yourselves into such trouble. Those who accept the great honor of taking part in the Council must be always at the disposal of the viceroy, day and night."

"Really?" asked the prince.

"Really. At his, or her, beck and call. Worse than a soldier. It is the fundamental requirement. And since you all declared you were not at her disposal, she now has the absolute power to replace you as she sees fit, whenever and however she wants. You've made a big—"

He was interrupted by the Chief of Ceremonies.

"Donna Eleonora wants to see you at once."

"Me?" the protonotary asked, surprised.

"Yes, you."

"Please excuse me," said don Gerlando, rushing off.

"Let's stay here another five minutes to discuss matters amongst ourselves," said the bishop. "Because I have the impression the situation is much more serious than we thought."

"Agreed," said the others.

As soon as they had all sat down, a captain came in. He clicked his heels by way of salute, but didn't look any of them in the eye.

"What is it?" the prince asked him.

"By order of the Viceroy, the entire palace, including the Hall of Council, must be vacated at once."

The Councillors began muttering to themselves, but it was no use protesting. They had no choice but to obey.

They stood up slowly, purposely dragging their feet as they descended the stairs in silence, then reached the courtyard where their carriages were waiting for them.

"This evening, an hour after sunset, we'll meet at my place," the Grand Captain said to the others under his breath, looking cautiously around, as they took leave of one another.

The table was set for three.

Donna Eleonora had wanted the protonotary and General de Timpa to stay and eat with her. Everything she said during the meal thrilled the general and scared the pants off the protonotary.

Not that the marquesa had shown any intention to act against the law. On the contrary, she wanted to play by the rules at all cost. Before doing anything, she wanted to know from him whether it was legitimate or not. And yet—and this was what frightened the protonotary—there was no question that what donna Eleonora had in mind would have grave consequences, the outcome of which could not be foreseen.

The general, on the other hand, could smell a battle in the air and was pawing the ground like a thoroughbred horse anxious for the race to begin. And he too was a bit taken by the marquesa. He had at last met a woman who, aside from having all the feminine attributes in the highest degree, also possessed a big pair of *huevones*.

When they had finished, donna Eleonora thanked them,

took her leave, and went into the private sitting room, where don Serafino, the court physician, was waiting for her impatiently, more besotted than ever.

"Can I count on *su confianza?*" she asked the moment she entered.

Don Serafino didn't answer. But he couldn't have even if he'd wanted to, since he was all choked up. He fell to his knees, eyes moist, took her hand, and kissed it.

Donna Eleonora told him what she wanted from him. Don Serafino listened carefully and then promised that he would do everything she'd asked within the time allotted.

An hour later he was dismissed, because the princess of Trabia, the highest ranking noblewoman in Palermo, had requested an audience. And donna Eleonora received her at once, because it was very important to have the support of at least part of the Palermo nobility in order to do what she had in mind to do.

The last thing she expected, however, was to find before her such a decrepit old woman. The years had reduced the princess to a sort of featherless little bird. She was all dried up, shrunken, and hunched over. But in the middle of the mass of wrinkles that her face had become shone two eyes with a still razor-sharp gaze. She leaned on a cane to walk and took offense if anyone made any move to help her.

She wore no jewelry. And to think that the jewels of the princes of Trabia were legendary.

"You are even more beautiful than they say," said the princess, sitting down. "And from what I hear you're also an exception."

She had a clear, gentle but firm voice, typical of one accustomed to giving orders.

"*Por qué soy una excepción?*"

"Because beauty and intelligence do not always go hand in hand. And I can tell that you're an intelligent girl. I am pleased for your sake, and for our country's."

Donna Eleonora took her hand and squeezed it in her own. She realized that the princess was someone who spoke her mind, who had on her lips the same things as in her heart.

"Was your grandmother by chance the Baroness Fabiana Contarello di Comiso, who later married the Marquis Ardigò di Nocita before they all picked up and moved to Spain?" asked the princess.

"Yes."

"I knew your grandmother well, and for a few years we were close friends. Is she still alive?"

"She died *cuando yo tenía cinco años*."

"Your grandmother Fabiana came to see me here in Palermo in forty-seven, the year the insurrection broke out. She was unable to return home and had to stay with me for a whole month."

All at once she started coughing violently. Donna Eleonora became afraid that the princess's fragile chest might burst. She got up to send for some water, but the princess gestured for her to sit back down.

"I wasn't coughing, I was laughing."

"*Por qué se ríe?*"

"I remembered something from a great many years ago." Losing herself in her memories, for a moment the sparkle in her eyes faded a little. Then she resumed speaking.

"You see, just before the uprising started, people in town were so hungry that the *buttane*—"

"*Buttane?*" donna Eleonora interrupted her, not understanding the word, which she'd never heard before.

"*Putas*. They no longer had any clients, poor things, and were dying of hunger and hardship. And some were even being raped and murdered. As is starting to happen again today. At any rate, about thirty of these women had taken refuge in the garden of our villa. And so I decided to feed them, at midday and in the evenings. I asked your Nonna

Fabiana to help me, but she was afraid to. She didn't want to have anything to do with them. Her confessor had convinced her that prostitutes had tails, like devils. But, after talking and talking to her, I managed to make her see that they were just like the rest of us women, and in the end she lent me a hand."

Donna Eleonora remained pensive for a moment, then said: "Yes, I have seen *mucha prostitución*."

"And there's more with each passing day. My son-in-law told me that nowadays they find old whores dead of starvation in the middle of the road, like dog carcasses. But the worst of it is that nobody wants to see it. A lot of women from good families are forced to sell themselves, but they do it in secret. Ah, the things I could do for these poor girls if were still young! I say this to you because you're a woman, and you understand."

At that moment donna Eleonora understood why the princess had called on her.

* * *

Bishop Turro Mendoza, too nervous to keep still, paced back and forth in the room, exhaling smoke from his nostrils like an enraged bull in the arena and waving in the air a letter consisting of a single line.

All the other Councillors had received the same letter.

The Holy Royal Council shall convene tomorrow morning at ten o'clock.
Signed, *the Viceroy, Eleonora de Guzmàn*

"Utter madness! Utter madness!" he kept repeating.

"A deliberate provocation!" don Severino shouted.

"As if we hadn't told her again and again that we absolutely could not do it tomorrow!" don Alterio said indignantly.

"Her purpose is clear," the prince of Ficarazzi intervened. "It's a test of strength."

"Meaning?" asked the bishop.

"Meaning that if we don't show up tomorrow morning, she will divest us of our functions."

"Ergo, we must show up," said don Cono.

"Ergo, my ass! Don't jump to conclusions! We're meeting here to think things over," said the prince.

"There isn't much to think over," don Arcangelo cut in. "We either go, or we don't go. *Tertium non datur.*"[1]

"In my opinion we should keep doing as we did this morning, all speak and act the same way," the prince retorted.

"To be honest, it's not as if the results have been so great," don Severino pointed out. "She took us by the hand and led us where she wanted. While we, all huddled together like sheep, we didn't understand a thing and fell right into the trap."

"At any rate," don Arcangelo said thoughtfully, "whether we show up tomorrow or not, sooner or later *la señora marquesa* is going to send us all packing just the same."

"And that could be a big mistake on her part, provided we remain united," said the prince.

"Explain," said don Alterio.

"There have been prior cases of a Councillor being replaced, but it's never happened that a whole Council was dismissed. We have the strength of numbers on our side."

"I don't understand," said don Alterio, who seemed unconvinced.

"Don't six heads reason better than one? We six can always say that the woman is mad, or acts as though she is."

"But to whom will we say it?"

"To His Majesty the King. As soon as she discharges us, we'll write to the King. We'll tell him that such a measure

[1] There is no third way. (Latin)

threatens to worsen an already grave situation and set all of Sicily ablaze. And, mark my words, His Majesty will call her immediately back to Spain. If we're members of the Council it's because we're men worth our weight in gold. We're hardly the bottom of the barrel, after all. It is we who uphold the Spanish monarchy here. Viceroys come and go, but we remain."

"You've almost convinced me," said the bishop. "But there's an immediate problem that must be resolved. What shall we do about the meeting convened for tomorrow? I have a suggestion."

"Let's hear it."

"We should go tomorrow."

The Councillors froze.

"What do you mean? We should throw in the towel?" don Severino asked feistily.

"No. We're not throwing in any towels. Listen carefully. Tomorrow we will enter the hall and sit down, and when she comes in, we will not rise, we will remain as still as statues. Without saying a word, without moving an inch during the entire session. Our bodies will be present, but our minds will not. And, you'll see: if she wants to get the message, she'll get it."

The Councillors, unable to restrain themselves, started clapping enthusiastically. The prince embraced them all.

The next morning, at ten o'clock sharp, the Councillors took their seats, their buttocks seeking the most comfortable positions possible, since they would have to remain that way for a few hours.

The protonotary and secretary took their places.

Some ten minutes passed, but nothing happened. Why the delay? This had never happened before. Then the Chief of Ceremonies appeared, stopping one step inside the hall.

"My lord Councillors," he said.

None of the Councillors made any move to turn and look at him. Their faces remained in profile. Only the protonotary and secretary were looking at him. This was not normal.

"My lord Councillors," the Chief of Ceremonies repeated.

Nothing doing. It was like talking to six statues.

The Chief of Ceremonies thought about this for a moment, then went ahead and said what he had to say.

"The *señora marquesa* sends her apologies, but she has no choice but to delay the start of the session by half an hour."

He waited for a reaction that never came. And so he exited and rushed to inform donna Eleonora of how the Councillors were acting.

The marquesa smiled.

Half an hour passed and nothing happened. Then, another fifteen minutes later, the Chief of Ceremonies returned.

"The *señora marquesa* begs the pardon of my lord Councillors, but for reasons beyond her control, she has no choice but to postpone the session until this evening, at sunset."

Five Councillors remained stock-still. Only one, don Alterio, shot to his feet to protest.

"No, no, no! I have an engagement this evening which I cannot possibly cancel!"

The unity desired by the Grand Captain had been broken. It had to be immediately re-established, otherwise it would become like a leak in a ship that might eventually cause it to sink. The prince turned to the Chief of Ceremonies and said:

"Report to the marquesa that the entire Council is unavailable for this evening."

As soon as the Chief of Ceremonies went out, the Councillors were finally able to take a break. The prince cleaned his nose, don Severino went to take a piss, the bishop scratched his itchy bottom, don Cono and don Alterio went for a little walk to stretch their legs.

The Chief of Ceremonies returned a short while later.

"The *señora marquesa* says that, given that it was her fault the session had to be cancelled, she would like their Excellencies of the Council to decide when they should next convene. I shall return shortly for your reply."

The Grand Captain asked the protonotary please to step out of the hall so that the Councillors could confer in private.

Finding themselves alone, with no outsiders present, the Councillors indulged in a revel of embraces and kisses and handshakes and pats on the back.

"We won! We won!" the bishop explained.

"Didn't I say that unity is strength?" the Grand Captain boasted proudly.

Don Alterio rubbed his hands together, happy as a lark, and said:

"I guess la señora has worked out who it is that gives the orders around here!"

"So, what day will it be?" asked don Severino.

"I," said the prince, "am of the opinion that things should remain as they are. That is, that the Council should continue to meet every Wednesday. Are you in agreement?"

The other Councillors were in agreement, and so the prince let the protonotary and secretary back inside.

Then the Chief of Ceremonies returned.

"Please inform the *señora marquesa* that the Councillors have decided that the next Council will be held next Wednesday at ten o'clock. Then return with her answer."

The Chief of Ceremonies came back almost immediately.

"The *señora marquesa* agrees to your terms."

The Concillors looked at one another in satsifaction. The marquesa had surrendered; the victory was total, on all fronts.

"Who will close the session?" asked the prince.

"Nobody," said the protonotary, "because this session was never opened."

* * *

At nightfall, the blazonless carriage of the house of Batticani pulled up, like two nights earlier, in front of the outlying palazzetto, and don Alterio told the coachman to come back and get him some three hours later.

Don Simone opened the front door for him with a smile on his face.

"My lord duke, you are always welcome here."

Don Alterio went inside, and the door closed behind him. The place was as quiet as the last time.

"I've heard the viceroy's widow is making things unpleasant for you."

"Yes, yes," don Alterio said, sighing.

He had no desire to talk or waste any time. He wanted only to dive between Cilistina's legs as soon as possible and stay there.

The previous night had been a terrible ordeal for him. He'd been unable to fall asleep, so great was his desire for her. Instead of blood running through his veins, what he felt was live fire. He'd tossed and turned for so long that at a certain point his wife had asked him what was wrong.

"I'm having trouble digesting the partridge."

And he'd kept on tossing and turning until donna Matilde finally got fed up and threw him out of bed. He paced back and forth through the house until dawn.

"Would you do me the honor of coming into my office for a moment?" don Simone asked him.

He couldn't refuse. So he followed him.

The office was a stuffy little room full of papers, with a tiny window.

"This is where I keep all the institution's accounts," said don Simone. "Unfortunately there's never enough money. The girls are still girls and have hearty appetites."

He sighed and then asked:

"Would you like a nice little glass of rosolio that the monks of Santo Spirito bring me from time to time? Friar Giovanni, the abbot, often comes to see the girls and give them comfort."

Why was don Simone wasting his time? What was the point of all this ceremony? Why was he drawing it all out? Perhaps it was best to accept the little glass and try to end the preambles as quickly as possible.

"Why, yes, thank you," he said.

The rosolio was foul. As he was drinking it, one drop at a time, don Simone grabbed a sheet of paper and showed it to him.

"Here," he said, "we have an early list of girls judged eligible to join our refuge. There are about twenty of them. And I can assure you that three or four are far better than those you've already seen."

"On what basis do you select them?"

"They're brought to my attention by village priests, parish priests, abbesses, nuns, friars . . . I only trust Church people in this; they really have an eye for women. And then I examine them one by one to see whether they have the . . . the necessary requirements."

He licked his lips, thinking of the examinations to which he'd subjected the girls.

"Would you like to come upstairs, my lord duke?" he asked the other.

"Yes."

Don Alterio found the stairs interminable, the corridor likewise. At last they came to Cilistina's cell.

"She's waiting for you," said don Simone.

"The key," said don Alterio, holding out a hand so shaky, it looked as if he had tertian fever.

Don Simone looked at the bunch of keys on his belt, and a furrow appeared on his brow.

"I can't find it."

Don Alterio tapped his foot impatiently. It didn't take much to set him off.

"Look a little harder."

Don Simone examined them one by one. It took forever.

"It's not here. Where could I have put it?"

Then he slapped himself in the forehead.

"Ah! This morning, when . . . It must be in my office. I'll go and fetch it. I'll be right back."

Don Alterio couldn't resist peering through the spy-hole.

Cilistina was lying naked on the bed, legs spread, hands behind her head and smiling at him. He got so lost gazing at her that he had no idea how long it took don Simone to return.

"I'm sorry, but for the moment I can't find it," he said with a sly grin on his face.

"What do you mean, 'for the moment'?"

"It means that I'll find it only when you've managed to have reinstated the donation that was canceled by donna Eleonora. Is that clear?"

Don Alterio immediately felt like killing him with his own two hands, then and there. So the son-of-a-bitch had done that whole song and dance to stoke his yearning for Cilistina? But what could he do about it? Nothing.

"Yes," he said through clenched teeth.

CHAPTER SIX

The "Holy Refuge for Endangered Virgins"

Having gone through a night even more wretched, bitter, and miserable than the previous one, don Alterio, after hours and hours lost ruminating over what to do until his head was about to burst, at dawn finally reached the only conclusion possible to avoid going completely insane or throwing himself out the window.

The solution was to go at once and talk to donna Eleonora in person, and try to persuade her to change her mind. At all costs, even that of selling himself to her body and soul and abandoning his friends on the Council. His very life depended on the marquesa reconsidering the request for a biannual subsidy for don Simone's refuge and giving a favorable response this time, retracting the cancellation that she herself had decreed.

It wouldn't be easy, that was more than certain, but there was nothing left for him to do. Or, at least, he could see no other way.

But might it not be better—he thought at one point—to write her a letter?

He gave this idea long and serious consideration but then decided that it was better not to. Written documents are always dangerous. How did the Romans put it? *Verba volant scripta manent.*

No, he was only wasting his time.

All he could do was summon courage from his desperation and call at the palace.

But would he be able to stand donna Eleonora's inquiring eyes? Would he succeed in telling her one lie after another while maintaining at all times an honest, loyal expression on his face?

Whatever the case, it was a very risky move, one that might cost him dearly.

For two reasons. The first was that he had no idea how donna Eleonora would react. She might have him thrown out of the palace with so many kicks in the pants. The second was the manner in which the other Councillors would take the news were they ever to find out. They would surely deem it a betrayal. And they would be more than right. There was no getting around it: by going alone to see donna Eleonora, without their knowledge, he would betray the agreement that they should all act in concert, as one single person.

But his lust for Cilistina, for her burning flesh, her velvety mouth, her silken thighs, her iron-hard breasts, was stronger than any misgivings.

He got dressed and went out, but decided not to take his carriage, preferring to go on foot. The cool morning air would do him good.

By nine o'clock he was inside the palace, telling the Chief of Ceremonies that he urgently needed to have an audience with donna Eleonora, adding that he should let her know that his request was personal in nature and had nothing to do with matters of the Council.

The marquesa sent word that she would receive him in the sitting room in half an hour. Her curiosity had been aroused by this surprise visit, in the morning no less. She hadn't expected it.

Don Alterio was shown in and started reviewing in his mind everything he wanted to say and how he should say it.

His heart was beating fast, and his head ached from lack of sleep.

But when donna Eleonora stood before him, having just got out of bed, which was when her beauty shone brighter than the morning star, he lost all power of speech and managed only to eke out a sort of doglike whimper and bow so low that he almost lost his balance and risked falling headfirst into a great somersault.

"I'm listening," the marquesa said with a serious expression, sitting down and asking him to do the same.

Don Alterio pulled himself together, lucidly aware that at that moment he was putting everything on the line. And suddenly, as if by miracle, the words started coming into his head, sure and precise, in perfect order.

"Do you remember, my lady, that among the measures we passed on the morning our viceroy passed away, and which you later annulled, there was one concerning don Simone Trecca, the marquis of la Trigonella?"

"I no remember," donna Eleonora said drily.

For a moment he felt like dropping everything and leaving, but he managed to bear up.

"It was a biannual subsidy that—"

"Is the marquis in need?" donna Eleonora interrupted him.

"No, not personally, no."

"Who, then?"

She seemed impatient.

"The subsidy is not for him, but for a charitable . . . "

The marquesa stopped him by raising a lovely, very long hand that spoke more eloquently than any mouth. The index finger remained extended with the others folded, then moved left to right and right to left, gently and harmoniously but still signifying "no."

"I am very sorry, *pero no puedo ayudarle.* I cannot turn back. ."

Desperate, don Alterio closed his eyes, reopened them, sucked air into his lungs, and summoned the strength to react. The voice that came out sounded vexed, halfway between indignant and moved.

"But then twenty-five orphan girls will find themselves thrown out on the street, without a roof over their heads, with nothing to eat, defenseless, prey to every sort of danger . . . "

Donna Eleonora looked at him questioningly.

"*Por qué habla de* orphan girls?"

"Because the refuge that don Simone Trecca founded—at his own expense, mind you, moved only by compassion and Christian charity—is devoted to saving the bodies and souls of young orphan girls who would otherwise be destined for ruin! They're all endangered virgins, as don Simone calls them, and he has spent his own inheritance to rescue them."

Don Alterio congratulated himself.

Indeed he'd noticed that the marquesa was looking at him intently. She'd become quite attentive, in fact. Apparently the subject was of interest to her.

"I didn't realize this," she said thoughtfully after a pause, as though reproaching herself.

Don Alterio had to make a great effort not to start dancing. He struck the iron while it was still hot.

"If he's denied the subsidy, don Simone not only will have to give up rescuing other orphan girls, as he has in mind to do, but he'll be forced, as I've said, to close the refuge. And what will happen to those poor girls then?"

At this point the marquesa, after another silent pause, said something he would never have expected.

"I want to see."

"Don Simone? Even today I can—"

"No. I want to visit *esto refugio*."

Don Alterio felt his heart sink.

If the woman set foot in the little palace she would immediately realize that the endangered virgins had already long succombed to the danger. And she would throw both him and don Simone in jail.

He broke into a cold sweat and didn't know what to say.

But donna Eleonora herself came to his rescue. She said she wanted to go to the Refuge *alla hora de comer*—at mealtime. Don Alterio would have to meet her the following day in the courtyard before midday. She would use the carriage she normally did when she went out of the palace anonymously. Don Alterio would act as her guide.

Once outside, the duke of Batticani dashed to don Simone's house and, panting heavily from having run, told him what he had done and of the dangerous decision that Eleonora had made.

Unlike the fretting don Alterio, however, the marquis didn't become the least bit discouraged.

"Thank for your ever so generous concern. I'll see you tomorrow, then, at midday," he said.

Don Alterio looked at him in shock.

"But don't you realize the woman will immediately figure out what's going on? How can you be so—"

"Have no fear. Leave it to me."

Don Alterio gave up. He felt dead tired.

The first thing don Simone did was race to the workshop of a master marble-cutter and gave him a commission. The job had to be finished no later eight o'clock following morning.

"But that means I'll have to work all night!" the master marble-cutter protested.

"Then work all night. I'll pay you well."

Afterwards, he went and spoke to Matre Teresa, the abbess of the convent of Santa Lucia, who was one of the people who would call to his attention any needy orphan girls, endowed, however, with those attributes he was looking for. Knowing full well how the girls ended up, she was paid in hard cash.

"I can give you eighteen," said the abbess.

"But I also need four nuns, who mustn't ask any questions, however."

"None of the nuns here ask any questions."

"And can I see these eighteen girls?"

"Please follow me."

The eighteen orphan girls in the convent's care were much to don Simone's satisfaction.

Another seven were made available by Patre Aglianò, who maintained a shelter for retarded and crippled girls. These even exceeded don Simone's expectations.

After dark the twenty-five girls living in the palazzetto were packed, along with their attendants and chambermaids, into six carriages and sent to don Simone's country house. The orphans would have to make do and sleep on the floor for a night. They were young, after all, and it wouldn't be too hard on them.

Their cells were then occupied by the twenty-five orphan girls provided by the abbess and Patre Aglianò.

The four nuns installed themselves on the top floor, where only the master seamstress remained.

The following morning, after a great general clean-up of the premises, don Simone conducted a dress rehearsal of the performance they would have to give for donna Eleonora. In the kitchen, meanwhile, three cooks brought in just for the occasion were preparing dishes fit for a king.

The first thing don Alterio noticed upon arrival was the inscription carved into the marble slab hung outside the great door:

Holy Refuge Of Endangered Virgins

"What an honor! What an honor!" don Simone kept repeating as he walked and hopped like a cricket while leading donna Eleonora and don Alterio towards the refectory.

"The girls are eating now . . . "

They went in. The orphan girls rose to their feet and started singing, under the direction of a nun.

Long live Lady Eleanor!
You grace us coming through our door!
We are but poor orphan girls
but wish you the best in the world!
Long live our lady Viceroy!
We wish you peace and love and joy!

Don Alterio looked on spellbound as they sang.

But what had happened to all the beautiful girls he'd seen sleeping? Before him he saw only twenty-five wretched creatures—young girls, yes, but one was toothless, another a dwarf, another was over six and a half feet tall, a fourth was crosseyed, a fifth was missing an arm, a sixth drooled like a crone, a seventh had the tremors, an eighth had snot running down her nose . . .

One couldn't really look at them long without a feeling of disgust, and yet donna Eleonora was clearly moved to pity. After the song, she wanted to taste the soup from the dish of an orphan girl, and found it excellent.

She went into the kitchen anyway, and then she visited the chapel, the sewing room, all the cells, and even the top floor.

When it came time to leave, she said to don Simone that she was satisfied and would take the necessary measures. He knelt down before her as though worshiping the Blessed Virgin herself, and tried to take her hand and kiss it, but donna Eleonora was quick to put it behind her back.

When she was back in her carriage with don Alterio, she sat for a while in silence. Finally, as they were pulling into the courtyard of the palace, she said only:

"*Muchas gracias.* Wednesday, at Council, I shall order *el subsidio para el marqués de la Trigonella* to be reinstated."

Don Alterio, for excess of joy, very nearly had a heart attack.

But before he made a move to step down from the carriage, she said something else.

"I shall expect you in two hours."

Good God! Don Alterio immediately fell from heaven into hell.

What did the woman want in exchange?

"I would like to know *la situación actual del* public treasury and how much *dinero* there is personally available to the viceroy."

Don Alterio heaved a sigh of relief. She merely wanted information that he, as Chief Treasurer, could give her. So much the better, since the matter wouldn't take up much of his time.

* * *

Two hours later, after donna Eleonora had received don Alterio's report and the duke had immediately withdrawn, she gave the order to admit the protonotary into the viceroy's study, which she had made into her own office.

She explained to him in great detail what she intended to say to the Council on Wednesday. The protonotary limited himself to making a few observations.

But when she came to the proposal that she reverse her annulment of the subsidy for the marquis of La Trigonella, the protonotary twisted his mouth visibly.

"*No está de acuerdo?*"

"With all due respect, no."

"*No está de acuerdo sobre el subsidio o sobre la procedura?*"

"I should point out that I know nothing about this Refuge and I don't know the marquis personally. But it is my duty to warn you that the procedure could prove dangerous."

"*Por qué?*"

"First of all, because the annulment has already been written into the record, and no revision would be considered legal or serious. Secondly because in that case all the other Councillors could demand, quite rightly, that you do the same for them and their requests."

He was right, of course. Donna Eleonora made a disappointed face, like a little girl who'd been denied a piece of candy.

"*Pero,* I want to help *el marqués!*"

Seeing her make that face, the protonotary felt his blood stir. He had to do something to make her happy again. He thought about this for a moment, and then said there was surely a solution to the problem.

Donna Eleonora asked what that might be. The protonotary replied that the only solution was for her to take the money for the subsidy from that set aside for her personal expenses and receptions. In addition, this had to be done through a motion made *motu proprio*, because in that case she would be obliged only to make it known to the Council, without having to ask for its approval.

Donna Eleonora smiled. She'd anticipated the protonotary's reply, and that was why she'd wanted to know from the Chief Treasurer how much there was available.

There was plenty of money, because during his two-year reign as viceroy, don Angel had spent hardly anything.

The princess of Trabia would be pleased when she learned what donna Eleonora had done for the orphan girls.

Meanwhile, there was another idea that had been percolating in donna Eleonora's head. She would discuss it with don Serafino when he came for his usual evening visit.

The protonotary had just left when the Chief of Ceremonies handed her a letter that had arrived from Spain bearing the royal seal.

She had so hoped it would come soon, and now here it was, in her hand.

After expressing his condolences and confirming the will and testament of her husband, His Majesty informed her that, in response to don Angel's request, which she'd renewed, and ignoring the rule dictating that a Royal Visitor should come to Sicily every six years, he'd decided to send don Francisco Peyró as Royal Visitor General, who would be landing at Palermo on the following Thursday.

He was just the right man for the task at hand.

Donna Eleonora felt her heart fill with joy and started singing quietly to herself.

Don Francisco Peyró had already been to Palermo four years earlier, as Royal Visitor General, and the memory of what he'd done was still alive and still inspired fear.

He was a man of about fifty of grey countenance and a bit shabby in appearance, quiet and melancholy. He looked like a third-rate clerk of no importance, whereas he'd proved to be a very dangerous man—honest, conscientious, scrupulous, and implacable.

Every Royal Visitor General took orders from His Majesty alone, answering for his actions only to him, and had full power over every authority except for the Viceroy. For that reason every door had to be open to him, every register ready for examination, every account made available for his scrutiny.

Availing himself of his powers, don Francisco had wanted to inspect everything, even the accounts of the Holy Inquisition, and spent days and days doing so, and in the end, fearing no one, he had punished all those who had strayed even a little.

Thus, without a second thought, he'd sent to jail the all-powerful, untouchable don Federico Abbatellis, count of Cammarata and Grand Harbormaster, proving that he'd used a great deal of the Crown's money for his own gain.

And he'd demanded the resignation of don Vincenzo Nicolò Leofante, another untouchable, from his post as Chief Treasurer, accusing him of being too open-handed with his friends.

In short, he'd done more damage than a wild beast, and by the time he returned to Spain, some fifty people, including high officials, vicars, tax collectors, and accountants, had ended up behind bars.

* * *

Don Serafino showed up with a small bouquet of wildflowers he'd picked with his own two hands and handed it to donna Eleonora without saying a word.

She thanked him and blushed slightly.

Seeing her blush, don Serafina, who was already red himself from the strong emotions he was feeling, began to turn purple.

Then donna Eleonora said:

"*Estoy un poco cansada.*"

She was tired? These words had the same effect on don Serafino as if she'd said she felt she was on death's doorstep. He leapt to his feet and started asking:

"What's wrong? What do you feel? A headache? Chest pains? Leg pains? Would you like to lie down? Would you like me to leave?"

Donna Eleonora smiled.

"Calm down. *Estoy sólo un poco cansada.* Don't leave. *Su presencia me da consuelo.*"

Don Serafino sat back down. Donna Eleonora closed her eyes, and he watched her, mesmerized. If he died at that moment, he thought, he would die happy.

She reopened her eyes and asked:

"Did you meet with that person?"

"Yes."

He was so spellbound he had trouble speaking.

"Do you speak with him?"

"Yes."

"Did he accept?"

"Yes."

"*Cómo se llama?*"

"Don Valerio Montano."

"Tomorrow I would like to meet him."

A t about four o'clock in the afternoon of the same day, at the little palace that had by now become the official headquarters of the Holy Refuge of Endangered Virgins, everything returned to the way it had been before. The twenty-five borrowed orphan girls were sent back to their convent and shelter, the twenty-five original girls retook possession of their cells, and the guardians and chambermaids moved back into their rooms. And one hour after sunset, don Alterio arrived.

Between the nervous tension he'd suffered and his no longer containable desire for Cilistina, he was now pale in the face, with dark bags under his eyes and an unkempt beard. He even felt a touch of fever. He'd told his wife he had to attend an important meeting and wouldn't be back until the wee hours of the morning. This time he could take all the time he wanted.

"Are you unwell?" was the first thing don Simone asked him when he saw him.

"I feel quite well, thank you," he said.

And he would be feeling a lot better in a few minutes. He could only hope don Simone didn't start in with his usual rituals of politeness. The marquis looked at him and smiled.

"Would you be so kind as to come into my office for a moment?"

Good God, what a tremendous bore! But he had to resign himself.

"All right."

"This time I'll have a little glass of rosolio myself. We must toast to the success of the Holy Refuge!"

Don Alterio had no choice but to swallow the liqueur.

"You've done a very great thing," said don Simone. "I hadn't expected as much, I assure you. And now you're in command here, I mean it. What can I do to repay you?"

"You know what to do."

Don Simone gave him a sly look.

"Do you still want Cilistina? Or would you rather change? Perhaps just this once?"

"I want Cilistina."

"I was expecting that. And you know what I say to you? You can have her," said don Simone. "She's my gift to you. She's yours."

He dug a key out of his pocket and handed it to him.

"I found it. It's the one to Cilistina's cell. I am a man of my word. You can keep it. That way you can come and go as you like, even when I'm not here."

Don Alterio couldn't hold himself back any longer.

"Can I go upstairs?"

"Didn't I say you're in command here?"

Don Alterio climbed the stairs two by two.

And he was so busy that night that he didn't hear all the traffic around him.

Indeed, the Marquis Pullara, the Marquis Bendicò, the Baron Torregrossa, and Canon Bonsignore—all people who had been frequenting the Holy Refuge since its foundation— had come to celebrate the event.

But as he was putting his clothes back on in the first light of day and getting ready to leave, Cilistina, who was lying on the bed, watching him, softly said something he didn't understand.

"Eh?" he asked.

She signaled for him to come closer, then held out her hand

and pulled him down towards her until don Alterio's ear was within reach of her mouth.

"You must help me," she whispered.

"What do you need?"

And he stuck a hand in the pouch where he kept his money, ready to give her as much as she wanted.

"I'm pregnant."

"Eh?" he said absentmindedly.

"I'm pregnant."

Taken by surprise, Don Alterio got upset. The news pleased him not one bit, because by now he felt that he owned Cilistina. And he certainly wasn't the one who had got her pregnant.

"Who was it?"

"How should I know? There were so many before you, my lord."

Don Alterio swallowed his bile. Didn't he know, after all, what trade the orphan girls of the Holy Refuge practiced? Don Simone used them to win powerful friends who would then lend him a hand in the legitimate and less-than-legitimate deals he had going.

"And how can I help you?"

"By getting me out of this place."

"Where do you want to go?"

"I don't know, but I have to get out of here."

"Why?"

"Because if I stay the marquis will have me killed."

Don Alterio balked.

"What are you saying?"

"It's true. I'm absolutely sure of it. Eight months ago Saveria got pregnant, and the marquis made her disappear. And the same thing happened to Assunta three months ago."

"But what makes you think they were killed? Maybe the marquis had them taken to a place where—"

"No, sir. All the girls here are convinced. He had them killed and buried here nearby, in the country."

"By whom?"

"You don't know them. They're a couple of cutthroats, Pippo Nasca and Totò 'Mpallomeni. The marquis uses them every now and then. Then he repays them not just with money but by making two of us available to them. And one day when Pippo Nasca was doing it with Ninuzza, he told her what happened to Saveria and Assunta. Listen, if you save me, I swear I'll become your servant for the rest of my life."

"Have you told anyone?"

"No sir. What, do you think I'm stupid? I only told Teresina, the blonde in the first cell. She's a friend of mine."

Don Alterio couldn't stay any longer. He had to go home. On top of everything else, seeing her so frightened rekindled his desire. If he tarried another minute, he would end up back in her bed.

"All right, I'll think about it."

"When will you be back?"

"Tomorrow night."

This annoyance was really the last thing he needed. While he didn't believe that the marquis had had the two girls killed, it was clear that he'd made them disappear to avoid trouble. Which meant that he would also make Cilistina disappear if he found out she was pregnant. And don Alterio did not want this to happen. Therefore, willy nilly, he had to get Cilistina out of there. But once she was out, where was he going to put her? Ah, yes! That's it! He could send her Scavuzzo, where he had a country house his wife never set foot in because she didn't like it. But Scavuzzo was far away. He could only go there twice a week, at the very most. Still better than nothing.

After sleeping through the morning, don Alterio ate and

went to see don Simone. He'd got an idea that he thought might solve the problem of Cilistina.

"To what do I owe the honor?" the marquis asked him, showing him into his sitting room.

"I have to ask a big favor of you."

"Speak."

"I want Cilistina."

Don Simone gave him a confused look.

"Don't you have her already?"

"I want her always with me. I can keep her at the house I have in Scavuzzo. And you can bring in another girl to take her place."

"If it was up to me . . . " said the marquis.

"Why, is it not your decision?"

"Until yesterday it was. But didn't you hear what donna Eleonora said to me yesterday?"

"No."

"She said she wanted a list of the names of the orphan girls in our care, and that I was responsible for them, and that no girl could leave the Refuge unless there was someone to adopt her, and that in any case the adoption request had to be submitted to her, so she could decide whether or not to grant it. Unfortunately I had the list sent to her just this morning, and I don't think your wife would agree to adopting her.

All don Alterio could do at this point was start cursing.

And he cursed even more when, upon returning home, he found a written request from donna Eleonora wanting to know before evening how much of a decrease in earnings the Royal Treasury could afford. But she didn't deign to explain why she wanted to know.

It wasn't exactly an easy thing to do. Don Alterio had to summon the help of the vice-treasurer, who arrived with a carriage-load of papers. Then he had to summon the vice-treasurer's assistant as well.

In short, he didn't come out of his study until after night-fall, but after sending his answer to donna Eleonora, he had a carriage take him to the Holy Refuge just the same.

* * *

By half past nine all the Councillors were already in the great hall.

They decided almost immediately to let donna Eleonora do the talking. That would make it easier to work out what she had in mind, and they could act accordingly.

As the session opened, donna Eleonora looked inquiringly at the secretary, who told her that the Councillors had not given him any questions to ask as to the order of the day.

Donna Eleonora understood the Councillors' maneuver, but played along.

She said she would submit to the Council's opinion two laws she'd decided to institute after hearing the opinions of a few of the people involved.

The Councillors exchanged some worried, suspicious glances. Who were these people with whom she'd spoken?

If that was the way it was, and the lady was conducting secret meetings and receiving information, advice and suggestions from outsiders, it meant that she was a slyboots and that they must keep her under strict surveillance from that moment on.

But the fact was that donna Eleonora was bluffing. Aside from the court physician, she hadn't met with anyone, but she had, on the other hand, been reading dozens and dozens of letters that had long been coming in for her husband and had never received any reply. And she'd also taken note of many measures that don Angel had intended to take if sickness and death hadn't prevented him.

The first law, she explained, was nothing new. It had been

passed in 1514 by Viceroy Ugo Moncada, then repealed some forty years later, and she now wanted to reinstate it.

This was the law of the so-called *patri onusti*, the "burdened fathers"—that is, those heads-of-family who had at least twelve children, and who had been relieved, without distinction between rich and poor, of certain heavy taxes and minor tariffs. She, however—and this was the novelty—wanted to reduce the number of children concerned to eight.

Did the honorable Councillors have any observations to make?

The prince of Ficarazzi asked a question: Since the decreased payment of those taxes and tariffs would mean less revenue for the public purse, might it not have been wiser to know first the Grand Treasurer's opinion on the matter?

Donna Eleonora gave a smile as sweet as honey and said that, being a wise woman, she had indeed made sure to consult with the Grand Treasurer on the matter.

All the Councillors turned and looked at don Alterio. Why had he not informed them that he had been summoned to the palace? Hadn't they made an explicit agreement?

Don Alterio threw up his hands as if to say he'd completely forgotten to let them know. Which was true, since at the time the only thing on his mind had been Cilistina.

Nevertheless, from time to time the Concillors continued to look over at him with suspicion.

Donna Eleonora moved on to the second law she wanted to pass. And this was something entirely new. In all of Sicily, but especially in the big cities, disputes often arose not only between the different trade guilds, but also within each individual guild, disputes that almost always ended in brawls with injuries and even fatalities. With this law, each trade, from silversmiths to butchers to coachmen to tailors to chicken-breeders to mattress-makers and so on, had to be represented by a consul whom the tradesmen would freely elect. All the consuls would then be under the jurisdiction of a Magistrate of Commerce, who would have absolute discretionary power to adjudicate all questions or disputes brought before him. His verdict would be equal to that of a court of law.

The Councillors were bewildered. They hadn't expected the marquesa to come out with such a complicated law. The first to realize that this new Magistrate would have the power to create good or bad weather over half of Sicily was Bishop Turro Mendoza.

He said that he thought this law was a good thing, but that one must reflect long and hard over whom to choose for the grave responsibility of such a position.

Donna Eleonora gave him the same smile she'd given the prince, and said that she'd thought about it long and hard and had found someone who for her was the right man.

"Could we know his name?" asked the Grand Captain.

"*Claro*. Don Valerio Mantano."

The Councillors froze.

Don Valerio Montano, baron of Sant'Alessio, was known to all of Palermo as a very honest, scrupulous, upright man who lived a secluded life and would never have accepted a public post. There wasn't much to say about him, but there was a great deal to say, on the other hand, about who it was who had given his name to the marquesa.

"And has don Valerio accepted?" don Cono asked, still in shock.

"He say yes to me in person."

How busy the little slyboots had been! And was she now drawing her sword, getting ready to strike? She had to be stopped once and for all, before she did any further damage. As a first step, they would have to post certain trustworthy persons outside the palace to know who was going in and coming out.

The last thing donna Eleonora did was to inform the

Council that she had decided, *motu proprio*, to grant a biannual subsidy to the praiseworthy, charitable Holy Refuge for Endangered Virgins of the Marquis don Simone Trecca, and that she would raise the money necessary from the funds available to the Viceroy for personal expenses.

She added that before materially granting the subsidy, she would have to have a certain test conducted, but she didn't specify what it would be.

Then she looked around and, since nobody said anything, she said:

"*La sesión ha terminado.*"

She stood up, and everyone else did likewise.

After descending the three stairs, donna Eleonora stopped, made a confused face and, lightly touching her forehead as if she had just remembered something, she said:

"*Perdón,* I almost forget. *Mañana, un Visitador General* is coming to Palermo."

The Councillors were flabbergasted, and immediately started exchanging confused, worried glances.

"But it hasn't yet been six years since the last visit," said the Grand Captain.

"*Lo sé,* but His Majesty *ha recibido mi solicitaciòn* to send him ahead of time."

And so it was she who was putting them all in danger. The slyboots was rolling out the big guns. But still, it might come to nothing. A great many Visitors General had shown themselves willing, after one day, to close one eye, and sometimes even both.

"Why didn't you tell us sooner?"

"It was not possible," donna Eleonora said blithely, "*porque vosotros* decided that the next Council meeting *sería para hoy.*"

And this was why she hadn't objected; so she could wait until the very last minute to inform them of the Visitor's arrival.

"Do you know who it will be?" asked the bishop.

"*Sí, lo sé. Mi parece que se llame* . . . his name is . . . *ah, sí, don Francisco Peyró.*"

And then she left, as the Councillors, upon hearing that name, collapsed into their armchairs one after another like ninepins knocked down by a ball.

The first to recover was the bishop, who ordered the secretary to bring fresh water for everyone. And when it arrived, they each drank a good pint or so, as if they'd been thirsty for days.

They had to confront this new development head-on, without wasting a single minute.

"If the protonotary and secretary would please step outside . . . " the bishop said.

"*Matre santa*, what will we do now?" asked the Grand Captain.

"We're sunk!" don Cono wailed.

"Fucked!" don Severino added for precision.

"The marquesa's intentions are clear," said the Grand Captain. "Summoning Peyró is like sending for the hangman. That guy won't hesitate a minute to send us all to jail. And when we're in jail the marquesa will replace us all with people loyal to her, and that'll be the end of us!"

"Well," said don Cono, "Losing my position would be bad enough, but as for going to jail, I really don't feel like it."

"Why, do you think I do?" said the Grand Captain.

"There may be a solution," said don Arcangelo, who up to that moment hadn't said a word.

"And what would that be?"

"Kill him the minute he steps off the ship."

"And the marquesa will be immediately convinced it was us who did it," don Severino objected.

"But I was thinking of something that would look like an accident. Such as setting up a phony brawl amongst some sailors, where one of them, by accident . . . ," don Arcangelo explained.

"I'm against it," said the bishop. "Not against killing him, to be sure, but because something like that must be well prepared in advance. It takes time, which we don't have."

"So what should we do?" the Grand Captain asked, going back to square one.

Silence descended. Nobody could think of a way out of their predicament. They felt like rats in a cage.

At that moment the protonotary came in.

"If my lords have no further need of my services . . . "

The bishop got an idea.

"Wait just a minute. I need to ask you something.

"As you wish, sir."

The other Councillors formed a circle round the bishop, full of hope.

"The question I want to ask you is hypothetical; it has nothing to do with us Councillors, because we all have clean consciences, so we're not afraid of the Visitor General. But, hypothetically speaking, if a Councillor were to find himself, as it were, in difficulty and wanted to wriggle out . . . "

"I don't quite understand," said the protonotary.

He'd understood perfectly well, but wanted to savor the moment a little.

The bishop took a breath and resumed.

"Let us assume a Councillor had done something he shouldn't have, such as a favor for a friend, and derived a monetary benefit from it, or received perhaps a gift, or profited from something that wasn't his own . . . What could he do to avoid having the Grand Visitor put him in irons?"

"Ah, now you're speaking clearly!" exclaimed the protonotary. "But let me think about this for a moment."

He sat down at his place and buried his head in his hands, as the Councillors gathered silently around him.

When he removed his hands from his head, he asked the bishop:

"Are we still speaking hypothetically?"

"Of course," said Turro Mendoza.

The protonotary buried his head in his hands again and stayed that way for a spell. So as not to disturb him, the Councillors breathed very lightly. The protonotary then looked at them one by one and said.

"There may be a solution."

"And what would that be?" the six said in unison.

"The law is very clear. It is written that the Visitor General has no power against a Councillor who, though he may have acted wrongly, resigns from his post before the Visitor's arrival. If, still speaking hypothetically, you told the marquesa before this evening was over that you are abandoning your office, the Visitor could do nothing to you. And now, by your leave, I must go."

He stood up and went out.

A very heavy silence descended. The protonotary's words had gone straight to the six Councillors's brains, but their brains refused to grasp their meaning in full. Then, finally, the meaning itself became clear and exploded inside their heads, leaving them all stunned.

"Ahh, good Lord, what pain!" don Severino Lomascio suddenly cried, bringing a hand to his chest and falling into the nearest chair like an empty sack.

He was writhing from the pain in his chest and short of breath. He might be having an apoplectic fit, but nobody paid him any mind.

Every one of them had his own ass to worry about.

"As far as I'm concerned, there's nothing to consider, not even for a moment, and I tell you I'm absolutely determined not to resign, even if I die," the bishop said firmly.

Don Alterio, for his part, gave the matter little or no reflection either, and joined forces with Turro Mendoza, going and standing beside him.

"Me too," he said.

"Well, for me there's nothing left to do but to tender my resignation," said don Arcangelo Laferla, frowning darkly. "Between losing my post and prison, there's not much choice."

"I agree," said don Cono Giallombardo.

"And I . . . I . . . will resign with you," said don Severino Lomascio, still writhing.

"How delightful! How delightful indeed! Apparently you

two are the only members of the Holy Royal Council with consciences clean as a looking-glass," was the Grand Captain's bittersweet, slightly menacing comment, addressed to the bishop and Don Alterio.

"It's not a question of having clean consciences," the bishop retorted. "We all know that even a ton of lye wouldn't suffice to clean the consciences of all of us in here. But I am convinced that don Francisco Peyró, though a man of determination, would never have the courage to set himself against the Holy Mother Church."

"You have a short memory," don Cono intervened. "Let me remind you that just four years ago, when Peryó audited the accounts of the Holy Inquisition and did not find them in order, he forced don Néstor Benítez, who was nothing less than second-in-command to the Grand Inquisitor, to resign and go back to Spain, where he was promptly arrested. So you can imagine how afraid he is of you, who are a mere bishop."

"Good God, you're right," said Mendoza, recalling the whole affair. His only justification for forgetting was that, although already a bishop four years earlier, he was in faraway Viterbo.

"And what about you, don Alterio?" asked the Grand Captain. "Who's protecting you? Care to tell us? Perhaps donna Eleonora herself, since the two of you have been meeting on the sly?"

Don Alterio, scared to death that the story of his private visit on behalf of don Simone Trecca and the Holy Refuge might come out, reacted loudly:

"I was summoned by the marquesa in my capacity as Chief Treasurer! And we only talked about numbers! And if I didn't tell you about it—for which I again beg your pardon—it is because I forgot!"

"You must admit, at least, that this little lapse of memory is a bit strange."

"But it's because these days I . . . have an illness in the family."

"But you too, my dear don Alterio, come hell or high water, will have to resign," said the Grand Captain.

"Why?"

"For the simple reason that we can't very well present ourselves to all of Sicily as five dishonest men and one honest man, now can we?"

"What does that have do to with anything?"

"It has everything to do with everything. At any rate, if you don't resign, don Francisco Peyró will be duly informed that you too, who claim to be so honest, have some skeletons in your closet."

"I have never taken advantage of—"

"We know. But you haven't been able to refuse your playmates a few little favors just the same. Shall I name a few names?"

"No," said don Alterio.

And he threw up his hands in resignation.

"All right, I'll resign."

"I have an idea, and I think it's a good one," the bishop intervened at this point, addressing them all, after stepping back to think it over. "Instead of sending the marquesa six letters of resignation, one for each of us, let's send her just one, signed by us all."

"Why?" asked the prince.

"Because in this letter we'll write that the only real reason for our irrevocable resignations—because they have to be irrevocable—is the intolerable affront the marquesa has made to our honesty by sending for the Visitor. By summoning him, she is saying she does not trust us, and this lack of trust is an insult to us. That way nobody can think that we're resigning because we're afraid of the Grand Visitor."

They all immediately came out enthusiastically in favor of his proposal.

"Let's write it at once," said the prince.

"Wouldn't it be better to give it a little thought first?" countered the bishop.

"No, we'll write it now and send it to her at once. That way she'll realize just how great and spontaneous our indignation is."

"All right," the bishop consented.

"Who'll write it?" asked don Severino, who had recovered and could now stand up.

"I will," said the Grand Captain, and he went and sat at the desk of the protonotary and secretary, where there was paper, a quill, and ink.

"Why don't we write it in Spanish?" don Cono suggested. "In my opinion it will have more of an effect."

"Does anyone here speak Spanish well?" asked prince.

It turned out that they could all get by speaking it, but writing it . . .

In short, they lost an hour before they'd even started writing it, and another three to finish it. Then they turned it over to the Chief of Ceremonies.

When donna Eleonora received the letter from the six Councillors, she was in the company of don Serafino.

"*Hemos vencido! Hemos fecho* clean sweep!" she exclaimed.

And, carried away by her enthusiasm for the victory, without even realizing it she grabbed the court physician's right hand between her own and pressed it hard to her breast.

Following this gesture of immense trust, don Serafino's face, in an instant, turned from purple to yellow, and then from yellow to a cadaverous white. Then his legs suddenly gave out, and while for a moment he was able to remain standing, he quickly could no longer keep it up and fell to the ground, unconscious.

"Un medico! Un medico!" a terrified donna Eleonora started shouting.

Estrella came running. But fortunately there was no need for her to run out and look for a doctor, because a minute later don Serafino opened his eyes again and apologized, feeling ashamed of himself.

"You scared me," donna Eleonora said, looking at him lovingly. "If I were to lose my only friend, *el único verdadero amigo que tengo . . .* "

Only with a superhuman effort was don Serafino able, this time, to avoid falling straight into a cataleptic state.

* * *

That same evening don Alterio rushed to the Holy Refuge, dying of hunger for Cilistina.

Before he went out, however, donna Matilde had made him lose time, raising a great ruckus the moment she learned that he'd resigned from his office. She'd been so proud to be married to the Chief Treasurer! And now, just because of a little Spanish trollop . . . And she'd carried on for so long that by the time don Alterio got to the Holy Refuge, it was already past nine.

As usual, he dismissed his carriage and then knocked at the door. But nobody came to let him in.

How could this be? It wasn't even ten o'clock.

He knocked and knocked until he finally realized that it was no use. But for nothing in the world did he want to give up spending the night with Cilistina.

So he decided to check and see whether everyone was asleep and, turning round the corner of the palazzetto, he went behind and headed for the marquis's little window. The shutters were closed, but a bit of light shone through. Without thinking twice, he bent down, felt around with his hand, grabbed a large stone, and banged it hard, with all his might, against the wooden shutters, making a loud crash.

"What the hell is going on?" the marquis asked from inside the room.

Don Alterio said nothing, but only crashed the stone against the wood again.

Don Simone opened the window, then immediately fell back and drew his dagger.

"Who are you?" the marquis asked, unable to recognize the person he saw in the shadows.

"It's me," said don Alterio.

"My lord duke! Your Excellency! Wait while I come and open the front door for you," said the marquis.

"No need for that," said don Alterio who, placing his hands on the windowsill, hoisted himself up and inside. His lust for Cilistina had made him feel as strong as when he was twenty.

Once inside, he saw that there was another person in the office, a shabbily dressed man with the kind of face that was best avoided at night, and in the daytime as well. The man was sitting there stock-still, eyes motionless and cold, like a snake's.

"This is a trusted friend of mine, Totò 'Mpallomeni," said the marquis. "I'm sorry for the inconvenience, but I was convinced that by now, given the late hour, you weren't coming this evening. And so—"

"Good evening," don Alterio cut him short, not wanting to lose any more time than he already had, and he went out of the room.

Don Simone ran after him.

"Wait! Where are you going?"

"Where do you think I'm going?" don Alterio replied without slowing his hastening step.

"Wait," don Simone insisted, grabbing him by the sleeve.

Don Alterio wrenched himself free of don Simone's hand, indignant, and kept walking.

"I've something important to tell you!"

"You can tell me tomorrow."

"Listen, my lord duke . . . "

Meanwhile they'd come to the bottom of the staircase, and don Alterio had to stop, because there was a man coming down the stairs.

As he passed them, the man asked the marquis:

"Where's Totò?"

"He's waiting for you in my office."

When don Alterio started climbing the stairs he realized the marquis had given up trying to bust his chops and was chasing after the other man.

Before opening the door, he got the urge to look through the spyhole. He recoiled.

Cilistina was standing naked, pale, and trembling beside a basin on a tripod, wiping her back with a wet cloth, trying to wipe some blood away.

He unlocked the door and went in. Cilistina turned her back to the wall.

"What happened?"

"Nothing."

"What do you mean, nothing? What's all this blood?"

"I said it was nothing!"

Don Alterio looked at the bed and saw that the sheets were also covered with blood.

"Let me see your back."

Cilistina pretended not to have heard him.

"I said let me see your back."

The girl still did not turn around, and so don Alterio grabbed her by the waist and forced her to turn.

Her back was covered with some ten or so small, not very deep cuts, made with the tip of a dagger to cause more pain than damage.

"Who was it?"

"Never mind."

"Tell me who it was or I won't help you."

Cilistina reluctantly gave in.

"It was Pippo Nasca. He wanted me tonight, and the marquis couldn't get him to change his mind. Pippo's a wild beast, and the marquis figured you weren't coming anymore, and so . . . "

It was the man he'd crossed at the bottom of the staircase. So that was why the marquis had tried to stall him; so he wouldn't go in when Nasca was still with Cilistina.

"Why did he use the dagger?"

"Pippo likes to do that when he fucks . . . "

Don Alterio, while appearing to stay calm, was actually in the throes of a furious rage. The girl belonged to him now, and the marquis couldn't just do whatever he pleased with her. He had to set things right.

"You keep washing yourself while I go and have a talk with the marquis."

"No! for heaven's sake!"

"Why don't you want me to . . . "

"Because then, after my lord leaves, the marquis will have me thrashed! My lord has no idea what that man is capable of! My lord must think only of how to get me out of here!"

Don Alterio spent the night tending the girl's wounds. And racking his brains trying to find a way to free her. But however hard he tried, he couldn't think of anything. Not until he was on his way home did he remember donna Eleonora's words to the Council, when she declared she would be reinstating the subsidy to the Holy Refuge.

She'd said that she would do so only after conducting an *inspección*. What kind of inspection?

If he could find out before it was done, he might have a good card to play against don Simone, and in exchange for some information he might be able to secure the release of Cilistina.

But how?

Donna Eleonora had never seen don Francisco Peyró in person. She'd only heard tell of him. She was curious to meet him. When the Chief of Ceremonies informed her that the Grand Visitor General had arrived and requested an audience with her, she said she wanted to see him straightaway in the sitting room. She wanted to have a tête-à-tête with him before the official audience.

The Grand Visitor General might be grand and a general, but he was still a man—a man who, in the presence of donna Eleonora's great beauty, felt his heart suddenly skip a few beats.

He made a deep bow, bent down on one knee, and said:

"My lady, please accept the honor on behalf of our beloved king."

"Please rise, don Francisco."

The Visitor stood up and gave her a baffled look.

"What did you call me?"

"Don Francisco."

"Why?"

"What do you mean, 'why'? Isn't that your name?"

"No, my name is Esteban."

This time it was the marquesa who was baffled.

"But aren't you the Grand Visitor General?"

"Indeed I am! And here is His Majesty's letter."

Donna Eleonora took it and opened it. In it, His Majesty informed her that unfortunately, don Francisco Peyrò had fallen ill at the moment of departure, and that he'd thought it best, so as not to lose any time, to send, in his place, don Esteban de la Tierna, a valiant, strict man who, if he wasn't just like don Francisco, he came pretty close.

Donna Eleonora wanted don Esteban to stay and dine with her. The other two guests were don Serafino and don Valerio Montano, just appointed Magistrate of Commerce.

They talked for a long time, even well after they'd finished eating.

The marquesa wanted don Serafino and don Valerio to think of some names of people who could become Councillors to replace those who had resigned. In the end, donna Eleonora wanted to be left alone with don Serafino. She wanted to ask him something concerning the Holy Refuge for Endangered Virgins.

As soon as town criers announced donna Eleonora's two new laws, and people also found out that she'd succeeded in obtaining the resignation of all the rogues and greedyguts on the Royal Council, three-fourths of the people who'd been against having a woman as Viceroy quickly changed their minds. This was a woman who knew what she was doing, and who could teach the men a thing or two.

Bishop Turro Mendoza, the prince of Ficarazzi, and don Como, running into each other by chance at a wedding, stepped aside to discuss the situation.

"Have you heard the news?" asked the bishop.

"What news? There's been so much . . . " said the prince.

"I was referring to the fact that the marquesa had scared the pants off of us by telling us that the Visitor would be don Francisco Peyrò, when in fact it's someone called Esteban de la Tierna."

"I knew that," said don Cono. "It's because don Francisco got sick as he was getting ready to leave."

The prince of Ficarazzi started laughing. Then, looking at the other two, he opened his mouth, brought his right hand to his lips, fingertips pinched together, and started shaking it back and forth.

"You swallowed it! You swallowed it!" he said.

"Why? Isn't it true?" asked the bishop.

"No."

"Then what's the real story?"

"Can you really not figure it out for yourselves? The good marquesa knew all along that this de la Tierna was coming, but she told us Councillors that it would be don Francisco. And we all fled in terror. Which was exactly what she wanted. In short, my good men, we've just taken it in the ass from a woman."

"If that's the way it is, she's a real devil!" the bishop commented.

"What can we do?" asked don Cono.

"I've been gathering some information," said the prince. "There's a variety of opinions about this Visitor. Some say he's a reasonable man, so to speak, while others say there's no hope with him. I'd like to find out in person whether—"

"Yes, but now the man can't do anything to us," the bishop interrupted him.

"Be careful. He can't do anything to you as an ex-Councillor, but as a bishop you're still fair game. Are the Cathedral's accounts in order? How about the diocese's? If donna Eleonora plants a seed of doubt in his mind . . . And then there's something very important the protonotary didn't tell us, but which I went and looked up myself."

"And what's that?" asked the bishop.

"While it's true that the Visitor cannot insitute proceedings against an ex-Councillor, he does have the right to demand the restitution of all inappropriately acquired money—and I mean all. Should the Councillor refuse, the Visitor has the power to expropriate."

"What does that mean?" asked don Cono.

"It means that if donna Eleonora feels like it, she can leave us all with barely enough clothes to cover our bums."

"*O matre santa!*" said don Cono, turning pale.

"*O madonna biniditta!*" exclaimed the bishop.

"No point in invoking mothers and madonnas," said the prince. "We need to take action, without wasting any more time. I have an idea."

The other two looked at him eagerly.

"Tomorrow I will invite this don Esteban to eat at my house. I will explain to him that we personally have no gripe with him, but with the marquesa who sent for him. That way, as we're talking, I'll see what kind of man he is and whether he's someone we can deal with."

"And what if we can't?" asked don Cono.

"We'll say a novena in the Cathedral," the bishop said bitterly.

As he was leaving his house to go to his former office as Chief Treasurer to withdraw the personal papers he'd left there, don Alterio had a faint dizzy spell.

Between Cilistina's ordeal, their resignations, and the row kicked up by his wife, he was at the end of his rope.

The dizziness would have been of no consequence whatsoever had don Alterio not happened, at that moment, to be on the top step of the fourteen stairs that led down to the courtyard.

He lost his balance and tumbled down to the bottom of the staircase.

And there he remained, crying out in pain. He couldn't move his left foot and was bleeding from a gash in his head.

To add to the chaos, donna Matilde came running, saw him and, while descending the stairs, misstepped and fell on top of him with all her two hundered plus pounds before fainting in turn.

T he court physician was sent for at once, but it took the hand of God before don Alterio's servants could find out that the doctor had gone off to the Cassaro and track him down.

Don Serafino examined him to verify that there were no additional injuries to other parts of the body, then applied a compress of herbs to his foot, which had sustained a simple dislocation, wrapped it up, then wrapped his head as well. Luckily the wound was rather superficial.

Considering his fall, he'd been quite fortunate.

Don Alterio wanted the doctor to stay a while and chat, but don Serafino told him that he couldn't because he had to return to the Cassaro, and in haste, to look for a midwife who he knew lived there, and bring her to the palace because she was needed by donna Eleonora.

Don Alterio was taken aback.

"So donna Eleonora's pregnant?"

"Come on! She's a widow!"

"Well, don Angel still could have, during his last few days on earth . . . "

"You must be joking!"

"Why, then?"

"I guess I can tell you, since, as the marquesa told me herself, it was you who went and persuaded her to grant the subsidy to don Simone Trecca for his Holy Refuge."

Don Alterio grew alarmed.

"Are you the only one she told I went to see her?"

"Of course. Donna Eleonora knows who she can talk to and who she can't."

Don Alterio calmed down.

"So what's this about the midwife?" he asked.

"This midwife," don Serafino resumed, "whose name is Sidora Bonifacio, is highly skilled at her trade and is the most honest, trustworthy midwife I know."

"And why would you need such a midwife?"

"She will be asked to verify whether all the orphan girls staying at don Simone's Holy Refuge are not only still virgins, but have received no other offenses in any other parts of their bodies. Know what I mean?"

"Clearly."

"That's what the marquesa wanted, and that's what will be. It's the condition she has imposed for the release of the subsidy. And she will not budge from this demand."

Don Alterio wanted to go deeper into the question. He found it quite interesting, and indeed it might prove to his advantage.

"Tell me something, doctor, man to man," said don Alterio. "As for virginity, I get it. It's easy to establish whether a girl's a virgin or not. But how can one tell whether there's been any offense to other parts of the body?"

"There's an ancient method that's not very scientific, but it's the only way, and Sidonia Bonifacio knows how to do it."

"And how does it work?"

"You take an egg, you boil it till it's hard, then you blacken one half with candle-soot, and then you ever so lightly introduce the smoked half in the presumably offended part of the body and delicately pull it back out."

"And what does that show?"

"It shows whether the inner folds have been forced."

"Ah, I see, thank you," said don Alterio, whose pains all

suddenly vanished. "When can I start walking again?" he continued.

"I'll be back tomorrow morning to make you a new compress, and I hope you'll be walking again the day after tomorrow, though you may need to lean on a cane." ·

But even if he had to crawl on all fours, don Alterio intended to pay a call on that stinking jackanapes of a marquis and lay down his conditions.

He now had the upper hand and would know how to use it. At this point Cilistina's freedom was guaranteed.

The following morning the doctor found don Alterio's foot no longer swollen, and so did not apply another compress. He only dressed it lightly, and also reduced the bandages on the duke's head. He told him he could get up and, for that first day, limit himself to half an hour of walking.

"When can I go outside?"

"Tomorrow."

"Were you able to find the midwife?"

"No, she's away from Palermo. She was summoned to deliver the daughter of Baron Pennisi. She'll be back in two days."

This was exactly what don Alterio wanted to hear.

And just as the doctor was leaving, don Alterio suddenly realized that he would never make it through the coming night without being able to hold Cilistina in his arms.

He decided to go to the Holy Refuge at nightfall, even if he had to lean on a cane and screw a hat down on his head to hide the bandages. He would sleep with the girl and not meet with don Simone until the following day.

After all, since the midwife wouldn't be coming with donna Eleonora for another two days, he had time.

But the devil put his personal touch on things, and in the form most congenial to him: fire.

Already donna Matilde, as soon as she'd heard that he would have to go out that evening after dinner, had raised the roof and busted his cojones into a thousand pieces as she tsk-tsked him to death at the table.

"But where do you think you're going with that leg?"

"And with your broken head!"

"Can't you see you can't stand up straight?"

"Can't you understand you're no longer young?"

Don Alterio pretended as if she wasn't speaking to him and kept right on eating, his only thought that he would shortly be leaving his house and running to Cilistina.

He'd just finished eating and was getting up from the table when Pippino, the major domo, rushed in.

"The kitchen's on fire."

Don Alterio ran off and could do nothing more than notice how high the flames already were. With the combined help of the household servants and those of the nearby palazzi, it took them almost till midnight to put out the fire, which in the meantime had also spread to the two rooms beside the kitchen.

And so don Alterio had to go hungry that night.

And since donna Matilde was convinced that someone had cast the evil eye on her house, she even forced him to kneel beside her for two hours, praying.

The following evening, however, one hour after sunset, don Alterio was knocking at the great door of the Holy Refuge. And as he knocked, he took out the key to Cilistina's cell. This time he was not going to let don Simone waste any of his time by standing on ceremony.

The great door opened. And he looked straight into the criminal face of Totò 'Mpallomeni.

He remained speechless for moment.

"Good evening, my lord," said Totò.

"Good evening," don Alterio replied.

He brushed past him as he entered, then headed for the stairs. 'Mpallomeni ran after him, passed him, then blocked his way.

"The marquis wants to talk to you."

"Get out of my way."

"The marquis wants to explain to you—"

"There's nothing to explain.

"Look, sir—"

"Get the hell out of here, bastard."

The other didn't budge, but merely smiled mockingly, as though daring him to try and get by.

All of a sudden don Alterio realized that what was happening was an exact replica of the scene of a few evenings before, except that in the marquis's place there was now 'Mpallomeni. Clearly he was trying to stall him because at that moment Pippo Nasca was fucking Cilistina and amusing himself by torturing her with his dagger.

For a moment that was the vision before his eyes, but then he only saw red.

When his sight returned to normal, Totò 'Mpallomeni was lying on the floor groaning and clutching his lower abdomen with both hands. The kick he'd just received had been sudden and violent, and the simultaneous cane-blow straight to the head had been so forceful as to leave him completely stunned. He hadn't the strength to react, not even when don Alterio bent down, took the dagger from his belt, and ran towards the staircase.

The door of Cilistina's cell was wide open and there was nobody inside.

The mattress was rolled up on the wooden planks, the sheets were gone, there wasn't a single article of clothing on the clothes rack. The room looked as if it had never been lived in.

He stood there, stunned, staring into the empty room.

A hundered different confused thoughts flashed through his head, each one worse than the last.

His final hope was that they had simply moved her to another cell, but he immediately became convinced that there would have been no reason to do so. Clearly the marquis had learned that Cilistina was pregnant and got rid of her. As he'd done with the other two girls.

But maybe he hadn't had her killed. He couldn't bring himself to believe that the marquis was capable of such a thing. That story of killings must have been a figment of the girls' imaginations.

He started slowly descending the stairs, thinking and trying to calm himself down.

He had to weigh his words, control his gestures, stay always lucid. Anger was his enemy; it could make him say and do the wrong things, all of which would harm Cilistina.

When he went into the marquis's office he found him there alone. Totò 'Mpallomeni wasn't there, though he was probably hiding somewhere, ready to come running when the marquis called for him.

Careful, Alterio, he advised himself. *Remember that Cilistina's fate is in your hands.*

He scornfully threw the dagger onto the desk.

"Give this back to its owner."

And he sat down in front of don Simone without saying another word.

Don Simone spoke without once taking his eyes off the dagger.

"I wanted to spare you this nasty surprise," he said. "But my lord refused to listen to 'Mpallomeni . . . You hurt him, you know. The poor man was just following my orders—"

"Where is Cilistina?" don Alterio cut him off, forcing himself to speak as calmly as possible.

The marquis threw up his hands and said nothing.

"Where is she?" don Alterio repeated.

"Will you believe me if I tell you I don't know?"

"No."

"And yet it's true."

"Why is she not in her cell?"

"She ran away."

"And how did she do that?"

"The person who locks the cells every night is a maid named Filippa. This morning the other maids noticed that Cilistina's door was open and her cell was empty. When they went to look for Filippa, she was gone too. She'd escaped with Cilistina."

"And how could Cilistina have persuaded her to do that? Certainly not with money, since she didn't have any."

"Apparently Filippa was in love with her."

The story made no sense. Don Alterio pretended to believe it.

"But have you looked for her?"

"Of course. That's all Pippo Nasca and Totò 'Mpallomeni have been doing since dawn this morning. Neither of them has seen her."

"Do you know whether she has any distant relatives?"

"Yes, a female cousin who lives under Mount Pellegrino."

"So one could—"

"We already have. I sent Pippo Nasca there. They know nothing. But tell me something. Did you tell Cilistina who you were?"

"No."

"So there's no chance you'll find her waiting for you outside your door."

He paused, and then continued: "I realize that you've become attached to Cilistina, but . . . you must set your heart at rest, my lord duke. I get the feeling we're not going to see that girl again."

The quick sidelong glance the marquis gave don Alterio

upon uttering these words made him absolutely convinced that Cilistina had been murdered, but he had the strength to remain impassive. Had he reacted badly and accused the marquis of murder, the man was capable of having him killed as well.

"At any rate," don Simone resumed, "you mustn't think that my debt to you ends here. You've yet to be repaid in full. If you'd like go upstairs and pick another girl . . . "

It suddenly occurred to don Alterio that perhaps some of the other girls had heard something that might help to find what had really happened to Cilistina.

"Now that you mention it . . . " he said.

"Bravo! That's the spirit! Come with me and I'll help you to choose."

"I've already chosen. I want the redhead on the second floor."

The redhead lived in the cell closest to Cilistina's. Don Simone made a face of regret.

"Ah, she's busy tonight with someone you know well, a colleague of yours from the Council."

It could only have been don Cono Giallombardo. In fact it was he who had first spoken to him about the Holy Refuge and explained how it functioned.

"Well, then, never mind," said don Alterio.

"I'm sorry you had to make this journey for nothing, my lord duke. But listen: I've been planning a nice big meal here for Sunday evening, to celebrate the granting of the subsidy. It'll be me, don Cono Giallombardo, Count Ciaravolo, Marquis Pullara, Marquis Bedicò, Baron Torregrossa and Canon Bonsignore. If you'd be so kind as to do me the honor, we could make it an even number: eight. With eight of the prettiest orphan girls of the Refuge. And those who wish to continue the evening alone with a girl will be quite free to do so."

Don Alterio pretended to think it over.

"All right. I'll come."

"Is your carriage outside?"

"No. It'll be back in a couple of hours."

"Then I'll have my own take you home."

"Thank you. And please do me a favor. You must tell 'Mpallomeni and Nasca to keep looking looking for Cilistina, when they can. And if they find her, or can give me some news of her, I'm prepared to pay them well."

"I'll tell them. But I don't think . . . "

Don Alterio likewise didn't think Nasca and 'Mpallomeni would be giving him any news of Cilistina. At the most they could tell him where they'd buried her. He'd said it only to convince the marquis that he'd swallowed the story about her running away.

The prince of Ficarazzi didn't manage to invite don Esteban de la Tierna in time, because don Estaban invited him first. But not to eat. He invited him to the palace, immediately, for a discussion. So immediately, in fact, that the officer and two soldiers who'd brought him the notice of summons waited for him to get ready, took him into the carriage in which they'd come, and brought him to a basement room in the palace where the Grand Visitor General had set up his office. The Visitor was sitting behind a table covered with papers and had a man at either side of him, two assistants he'd brought with him from Spain. As soon as don Giustino came in, don Esteban stood up, approached him, smiling, and sat him down in an armchair opposite his worktable.

Seeing him so affable, the prince perked up.

Don Esteban, for his part, after apologizing for disturbing him, pointed to the papers and said he'd been studying the appropriations made by the prince in his function as Grand Captain of Justice and had found them to be perfectly in order, immaculate.

The prince secretly breathed a sigh of relief. He was certain he'd left no written trace of his misdeeds, but one never knew.

Don Esteban continued, saying there was just one thing that was a wee bit unclear. But it was a trifle of no importance, which he was sure his excellency the prince could explain.

"I'd be happy to do so."

Did his excellency the prince have any recollection of what had happened at Roccalumera four months after the arrival of the late viceroy don Angel, rest his soul?

The prince replied that he didn't have a clear memory of it. He vaguely recalled that it had involved a popular uprising against—

Then—don Esteban interrupted him—by his excellency the prince's leave, he would refresh his memory by citing the report that he, as Grand Captain, had made to the late Viceroy. Was that all right?

Quite all right, said the prince.

So, according to the report, the population of Roccalumera, led by an important cloth merchant by the name of Angelo Butera, had risen up against Count don Vincenzo Aricò di Santa Novella, the lord of the town, because the count's twenty-year-old son, Jacopo, had, for no reason other than the pleasure of doing so, had an old peasant bludgeoned to death. But his excellency the prince, when he got to the site of the unrest after the revolt had been firmly put down, declared that things were not as had been reported. That is, the old peasant died because he'd fallen to the bottom of a ravine, and Angelo Butera had made up the whole story of the beating, inciting the population against don Vincenzo and his son because of a row over an expensive lot of oriental fabric that Jacopo had ordered and refused to pay for when he found it not to be first-rate, as their agreement had stipulated. And, as a result, he, the prince, had had the merchant arrested and thrown in jail, where he still remained. Was this what happened?

Of course that was what happened. He now remembered perfectly well.

So his excellency the prince confirmed this account?

He did.

Very well, then don Esteban had some news for him. Did he know that Jacopo, the twenty-year-old son of don Vincenzo Aricò, was killed in Catania four months following those events?

The prince knew this.

And did he know that don Vincenzo had died three months later, from heartache due to the loss of his son?

The prince knew this too.

But perhaps he did not know that don Vincenzo Aricò, as he was dying, had written a letter to don Angel—a letter that don Angel had never read, as he was already very sick. But donna Eleonora did read it.

And did his excellency the prince want to know what the letter said, unless of course this might disturb him?

His excellency the prince wanted to know, though purely for the sake of curiosity, given that he'd already resigned and, according to the law, could not be prosecuted in any way for any mistakes he might have made when in office.

"Here is the letter," said don Esteban, picking it up from the table and showing it to him. "Don Vincenzo confesses that the uprising broke out because his son, Jacopo, had had kidnapped and murdered—after having abused her at great length—the daughter of the merchant Angelo Butera. And that you, my lord prince, concocted a different story together with him, in exchange for three large sacks of gold coins. Along with the letter, don Vincenzo attached the testimony of his major domo, Nino Scileci, who'd gone materially to get the bags of money and was in the room when they were turned over to you. It is my duty to inform you, my lord prince, that yesterday evening this major domo, in person, and in our presence, verbally confirmed what he had written. And he submitted to us an empty sack identical to those in your possession. In conclusion, I cannot send you to jail, as you deserve, but I can require you to pay back three times the value of the three sacks of gold pieces."

"Why three times?" the prince, more dead than alive, managed to ask in a feeble voice.

Don Esteban made a little smile.

"It's true, you don't know yet. There is a new law, issued just this morning by donna Eleonora, which modifies the prior one. It also provides for the arrest of anyone who tries to avoid payment. You can go home now. You have one week to pay up. Tomorrow morning I shall let you know the exact amount you owe. We have to make some calculations. And I repeat: do not try to escape. You will be caught and arrested. You can go now."

Don Giustino did not stand up, and did not look at him.

The prince left the palace walking like a drunkard, bracing himself against the walls to keep from falling. Not even if he sold the castle of Ficarazzi, the fief of Petralia, and his palazzo in Palermo could he scrape together enough money. One hour earlier he'd entered the palace a rich man, and he now was leaving it poorer than a beggar.

It was only around the first light of dawn, when he put his mind at rest by accepting that Cilistina was now lost to him forever, that don Alterio had a clear idea of what he wanted to do and had to do. And everything he wanted and had to do could be summed up in a single word: revenge. But he couldn't understand—since it was of no importance whatsoever—whether he wanted to take revenge for Cilistina's murder or because don Simone had wounded his pride.

Then, as if relieved of a great weight, he immediately plunged into a deep sleep.

He woke up with donna Matilde shaking him, saying it was time to eat. It took great effort to open his eyes.

"I'm not hungry," he said.

"Do you feel unwell?"

Good God, what a pain!

"I feel fine."

"So why do you want to stay in bed?"

In his mind he cursed the saints, because if his wife found out, he would be forced to kneel down at once and beg forgiveness of the Lord.

"Look, I'll get up in a minute. Did the tailor bring the new clothes?"

"Yes, this morning."

"Have some hot water prepared for me."

When Pippino told him the water was ready, he went into

the lavatory and stayed there for an hour, washing himself inch by inch. Once he'd finished, he felt the need to wash himself a second time.

He put on his new clothes and went out. He told his coachman to take out the most elegant carriage, the one with the ducal crest in gold, and to drive him to the palace. When he climbed inside, he lowered the curtains so that he could think, one word at a time, of what he would say to donna Eleonora.

All of a sudden the carriage stopped. Perhaps an obstacle, he thought.

But a moment later the door opened, a man rushed in, sat down beside don Alterio, and closed the door behind him.

It was don Severino Lomascio, pale and frighted.

"I was passing by in my carriage, and when I saw yours, I hailed it," he said.

Don Alterio noticed that he was trembling.

"What's happening to you?"

"I'm fleeing Palermo."

"Why?"

"They're looking for me."

"Who is?"

"The Grand Visitor's guards. They're after me because I didn't show up at my appointed meeting with him this morning."

"And why didn't you show up?"

Don Severino looked at him in shock.

"What kind of question is that? Haven't you heard?"

"No, what should I have heard?"

"Didn't you hear that yesterday, in barely two hours, don Esteban reduced the prince of Ficarazzi to total poverty and madness?"

Now it was don Alterio's turn to be shocked.

"Really?!"

Don Severino told him the story.

"But you won't solve anything by running away. The man will expropriate your possessions whether you're here or not."

"In the meanwhile just this morning I sold two of my fiefs and my house here in town to don Onofrio Sucata and had him pay me in hard coin. I took a big loss, but it's still better than nothing. I'm going to go and hide in a really out-of-the-way place near Girgenti, where they won't find me even if they come with dogs. And what do you intend to do?"

"When he calls me, I'll go."

"Good luck," don Severino said to him, getting out of the carriage.

"Thanks, I really need it," don Alterio said to himself as his carriage started moving again.

It was just before ten o'clock, and they were in the sitting room of the private apartment, with donna Eleonora in an armchair and don Alterio standing in front of her.

The marquesa had invited him to sit down, but he refused, standing stiffly before her like a soldier—even though his legs were shaking a little.

"If I've understood you correctly," said donna Eleonora, who for the fifteen minutes in which he'd been talking had maintained the same expression of near total indifference, "when you came to talk me into granting the *subsidio* to the *Sagrado Refugio,* did you already know for what horrible purpose the orphan girls were put there?"

"Yes, I knew."

"And when you came with me to the *refugio* and realized the trick that don Simon was playing, you said nothing?"

"That's right"

"And you did all this *por una malsana pasión* for one of the orphan girls?"

"Unfortunately, yes."

"And you suspect that *el marqués* sent someone *a matar a dos huérfanas, y a la chica de la que Usted estaba enamorado*, because they were pregnant?"

"I have reason to believe that is what happened."

"And this Sunday night there will be *una fiesta particular* at the *refugio,* among eight of the refuge's regular patrons?"

"Yes."

"Are you aware of the *irremediables consecuencias* your words may have for you?"

"I am perfectly aware of them."

"Do you have any *remordimiento* for what you have done?"

"No."

Donna Eleneora remained silent for a long time. Then she said:

"I must now ask you a question that will be difficult to answer, *ya lo sé.* But you must answer *sinceramente.*"

"Go ahead."

"The first time the Council voted in favor of *el subsidio al marqués,* did everyone already know that my husband, the viceroy,, *estaba muerto?*"

Don Alterio's gullet was as dry as the desert.

He wanted to say yes, but no voice came out.

He nodded his head affirmatively.

"One last question—and *mi decisión* will depend on your answer. Why are you doing all this?"

Don Alterio ran his parched tongue over his parched lips. He could have invented a hundred and one reasons, but with this woman it was best to be sincere.

"For revenge," he said.

Donna Eleonora stood up ever so slowly.

She was now a little pale, but her voice was the same as always, calm and harmonious. She looked don Alterio in the eye.

Is there such a thing as a black flame that flashes dark and violent? For a moment he saw just such a mysterious flame burning in the marquesa's pupils. And he felt more afraid than he ever had before in his life.

"I understand how you feel," said donna Eleonora. "Because I'm taking my own steps towards revenge. You men of the Council mocked a dead man and took shameless advantage of *el cadáver de mi esposo. Jamás se lo perdonaré.* My revenge on you will be to deny you your revenge."

Upon hearing these last words don Alterio felt himself dying. So it had all been pointless. Had he ruined himself for nothing?

"But I won't do it," the marquesa continued. "You shall have your vendetta. *Con una condición.*"

"What?"

"That on Sunday night you take part in this *fiesta.*"

"I'm sorry . . . but, I no longer want to set foot in there."

"But you must."

"Why?"

"I don't think *los presuntos caballeros* who will taking part in the fiesta with the eight orphan girls can be charged with anything. The only one who will be placed under arrest will be the marquis. I, however, *con toda mi fuerza,* want to subject the eight of you *a la ignominia general,* so that your illustrious names will be mud, *para siempre.*"

"I'll do as you ask," said don Alterio.

That evening a rumor spread that don Severino Lomascio had been arrested trying to flee and because of this had been put in jail. There was also news that don Arcangelo Laferla, former Admiral of the Fleet, after being given the third degree by the Visitor General don Esteban, had been reduced to begging for alms on the streets. All his estates, and there were many, had been exprorpriated.

On the occasion of the first meeting of all the consuls of the guilds, don Valerio Montano announced a new law promulgated by the Viceroy, donna Eleonora.

The law—called the law "of the three thirds"—determined that anyone who had any work done by people belonging to the guilds had to pay a third of the estimated cost at the start of the work, another third halfway through, and the last third at the end. Thus it became no longer possible for the nobles, the rich, and the well-off to pay for labor whenever they damn well pleased or to pay only half or even not to pay for it at all, as often happened.

The consuls were thrilled and called for a large demonstration of thanks on Sunday morning, at ten o'clock, to be held outside the palace.

And since in the guilds there were a great many *patri onusti*, the word got around and all the "burdened fathers" of Palermo decided to take part in the celebration of thanks.

That same day donna Eleonora received, in the Hall of Council, the six people who had agreed to become the new Councillors. They had been chosen one by one by don Serafino and don Alterio, and were all men whose honesty and rectitude were above suspicion.

They were: Monsignor Don Benedetto Arioso, bishop of Patti; don Filippo Arcadipane, prince of Militello, Grand Captain of Justice; don Sebastiano Consolo, duke of Scianò, Grand Treasurer; don Gaetano Currò, marquis of la Fiumara, Judge of the Monarchy; don Michele Galizio, count of Sciacca, Admiral of the Fleet; and don Artidoro Giummara, baron of San Michele, Chief Administrator. The current protonotary and secretary were reconfirmed in their positions and witnessed the six Councillors' bows of obeisance.

It was determined that the Council would meet twice a week, on Tuesdays and Wednesdays.

At four o'clock that afternoon, members of all seventy-two of the city's guilds and one hundred and eighty "burdened fathers," all with their wives and children, gathered in the square outside the Palazzo.

Never had so many people been seen all together like that, and strangest of all, so happy.

There were a few scrolls held aloft with wooden poles. The biggest one said:

Palermo reborn! The time has come!
We thank our Lady all and one!

Some shouted out loud: "Long live donna Eleonora!" Some cried: "We are all with you!" But then, little by little, all the different voices became a single chorus:

"Come to the window! Come to the window!"

Donna Eleonora, who was watching, unseen, from a half-shuttered window, had no desire to come out into the open. It was the Chief of Ceremonies who finally persuaded her.

"If you don't, they won't go away," he said.

Donna Eleonora opened the shutter and came to the window.

As soon as the people saw her they were dumbstruck, dazzled by her beauty.

A silence so total came over the crowd, it was frightening. Indeed, someone who couldn't see well asked fearfully:

"What happened? What happened?"

One second later a roar went up from the crowd, making the earth quake.

* * *

Bishop Turro Mendoza also quaked when he heard what had happened in front of the palace. By this point the marquesa had all of Palermo in the palm of her hand. And surely it was only a matter of days before he was summoned by the Visitor General, who would pick him clean.

And so he made a sudden decision. And a dangerous one. But, with nothing left to lose . . .

Thus, at midday Mass, with the faithful crammed into the Cathedral—which was something of a surprise, since it was not any special feast day—the flock watched him step up into the pulpit.

The bishop began by saying he wanted to open the eyes of the good people who were falling into a perilous trap laid by the Evil One. He said that the devil might be depicted with horns and a tail but that he very often changes aspect and can take on the appearance of an average gentleman or, worse yet—and this was something that happened more often—that of a very beautiful woman of angelic appearance.

And not only did this devil in woman's guise possess the power of beauty, but she also came across as a person of noble sentiment, generous and anxious to do good.

"With a woman like that, it's as if she is offering you a basket full of fresh, delicious fruit. You poor folk, how could you know it's a trick? And so you give thanks, and you reach out and take one of the fruits. How good it tastes! So you want another. And so you reach out again, and you don't see that this time, hidden at the bottom of the basket, is a poisonous snake, which bites your finger. You pay no mind to it, but meanwhile the devil's poison has entered you, and there's nothing more to be done. Now you, my faithful, you may be asking yourselves: How can he speak that way about a woman who is doing things for our betterment?

"And so I now ask you: How is it that this person, in all the time she's been here—and it's been more than two years—has never once, never, felt the need for a confessor? Does that seem right to you? I ask this of you, who confess and take communion regularly.

"And I ask as well, how is it that our late Viceroy was in fine health until the day she arrived, and then started to get sick?

"And finally, why does she keep her husband's dead body in a room inside the palace and doesn't want him given a proper Christian burial? Do you know how much the souls of the dead suffer . . . "

He interrupted himself for a moment, because an idea had flashed through his head, and then he resumed in conclusion:

" . . . how much the souls of the dead suffer when they are left without a prayer, without a Mass? These are the things I want you to reflect upon. And, like good Christians, you should have your friends reflect upon them as well, those who are unable to be here."

Having finished his sermon, he went into the sacristy and told his secretary to go and send at once for Don Asciolla, the priest of the palace chapel.

He must come at once, without a moment's delay. They would wait for him at the bishop's palace.

Going into his office, the bishop sent for Don Scipione Mezzatesta, a young priest whom he'd used in the past for certain matters better left unsaid. If they were ever to become known, they would certainly both end up in the clutches of the Holy Office.

He told him what he wanted from him. And Don Scipione replied that he was ready and able, as always.

With Don Asciolla, the bishop was curt and brusque.

"Has donna Eleonora come to the chapel today?"

"No, your excellency, she has never set foot in there."

"Have you tried to persuade her that, if she can't be bothered to take Communion, she should at least come on Sundays to hear the Holy Mass?"

"Never, your excellency."

"And why not?"

"Because it's no use, with that woman."

"Well it's no use with you either, Don Asciolla. I'm transferring you here, effective immediately. Don Scipione will be taking your place at the palace chapel."

Towards nightfall, on the sly, some forty soldiers under the command of Captain Miguel Ortiz entered the area around the little palace of the Holy Refuge and took up positions. The captain found a spot from where he could keep an eye on the main door, and started counting the carriages that arrived and then left without their occupants. When the seventh one had come and gone, he knew that all the guests were now there, since the marquis had already been inside for some time.

Now all they had to do was wait.

After more than an hour had gone by, and it was completely dark outside, two carriages arrived and stopped a short distance away. Out of the first stepped the Grand Captain of Justice in person, don Filippo Arcadipane; in the second sat the midwife, Sidora Bonifacio with two assistants, Maria and Cuncetta. Maria was holding a basket containing thirty hard-boiled eggs and five candles.

Meanwhile, inside, in the refectory, the great feast and drunken revel unfolded in a general atmosphere of good cheer and amusement. Even don Alterio pretended to take part in the festivities, though he was sick at heart.

Each guest had a girl at his side who saw to fetching dishes from the kitchen and keeping the jugs of wine always full.

Don Simone had also had the splendid idea to have the eight girls dress up as nuns, with nothing on underneath. And in each nun's habit four holes had been made: two with the breasts popping out, the third granting easy access to the little thicket and the valley below, and the fourth, which was in back and the largest, allowing one to caress the full moon with the utmost convenience.

"How do you plan to proceed?" don Filippo asked the captain.

The officer replied that he would first have the little palace surrounded, to prevent anyone from escaping, and then he would knock.

"But what if they don't answer?"

In that case he would break the door down.

"But that will remove the element of surprise! They'll have all the time in the world to put themselves back together!" said don Filippo. "Wouldn't it be better to send one of your experienced soldiers to see whether there is a way to get inside the house without breaking down the door?"

The captain agreed and sent a sergeant who was an old war-horse.

The sergeant returned half an hour later with good news. Which was that the main door was ajar and there were two men standing guard.

He said to the captain that if he gave him three soldiers of his own choice, he could guarantee him that the two guards would be seized and prevented from sounding the alarm.

And so it was that Pippo Nasca and Totò 'Mpallomeni, in the twinkling of an eye, found themselves put out of commission by two sharp blows to the head that seemed to have rained down from the sky.

Ten minutes later, don Filippo Arcadipane, the captain, and ten armed soldiers walked through the main door of the little palace.

"Nobody move," said don Filippo, entering the refectory.

Needless words, since everyone in the room had frozen. Don Simone while sinking his teeth into a chicken breast, Baron Torregrossa as he was bending over to kiss the tits of the girl sitting beside him, Canon Bonsignore as he was turning his attention to the full moon of a girl forced, for this purpose, to stand as she ate . . .

The first one able to react was don Cono Giallombardo.

"This is a private gathering. You have no right to arrest me!"

At that point, they all snapped out of it.

"You don't know who I am!" bellowed Count Ciaravolo.

"We are not doing anything illegal!" yelled Marquis Pullara.

"This is an outrage! You have no right!" said Marquis Bendicò, laying it on.

"Until a moment ago I indeed would have had no right," the Grand Captain replied frostily. "I could only have arrested the Marquis Trecca for running a brothel and calling it a charitable institution. But now I'm in a position to arrest you all."

"Why?" asked don Cono.

"Says who?" the Baron Torregrossa said belligerently.

"Says the law. You were all caught committing acts of willing, patent blasphemy, by obscenely using nuns' garments for lascivious ends. And on top of that, every feigned nun is wearing a crucifix round her neck."

It was true. Everyone fell silent.

"It's up to you to choose: either you let me arrest you, or I turn you over to the Holy Office," don Filippo continued.

Not one of the eight men had the slightest doubt as to his preference, and none put up any resistance when the soldiers tied their hands behind their backs.

The captain, meanwhile, accompanied the girls back to their cells.

Ten soldiers, under the command of a sergeant, stayed behind at the refuge. Don Filippo likewise.

The eight arrested gentlemen, together with Totò 'Mpallomeni and Pippo Nasca, headed off on foot to prison, under military escort.

Don Alterio wept as he walked. They were not tears of shame or despair, but liberating tears, almost tears of relief.

After they'd gone, the midwife and her two assistants entered the refuge with their basket of thirty eggs. The midwife began her examinations.

When she came back downstairs an hour later, she said she did not find a single orphan girl who was still a virgin. And therefore there was no need for the eggs.

The Grand Captain had her sign a paper and then left, as did the midwife and her two helpers. The ten soldiers stayed to guard the place.

Three hours later Pippo Nasca and Totò 'Mpallomeni confessed to having killed three orphan girls, as ordered by don Simone.

And they also said were they had buried them.

CHAPTER ELEVEN
Don Angel's Ghost Appears and Does a Lot of Damage

T he first session of the new Council opened punctually at ten o'clock on Tuesday morning.

The first to speak was the Grand Captain of Justice, who recounted what had transpired at the little palace of the Holy Refuge, and why he'd had to arrest everyone. Following the two assassins' confessions, he'd sent some soldiers to look for the three girls' corpses, which were found just a short distance from the Refuge. The bodies were then put in coffins and reburied in consecrated ground.

That morning the Tribunal decreed that the property of all the defendants would be confiscated, and they were sentenced to five years in prison, with the exception of don Simone, who was condemned to death, along with Nasca and 'Mpallomeni, for the triple murder.

The twenty-four orphan girls, upon the specific order of donna Eleonora, were taken to the convent of Santa Teresa.

The prior evening, after the full confession of don Simone, the accomplices who had pointed out the prettiest orphans for consignment to the brothel were also arrested. These included Matre Teresa, the abbess of the convent of Santa Lucia, Suor Martina, head of the orphanage run in conjunction with the convent of the Sacred Heart, Don Aglianò, who ran a shelter for orphan girls, and Brother Agenore, the assistant superior of the Franciscans.

The Grand Captain finished by saying that the marquis had submitted a list of the possessions he'd obtained through his shameful business practices, and the results were astonishing.

After him the Chief Administrator proposed that don Esteban, once he'd finished dealing with the former Councillors, should be transferred to Messina to put some pressure on the chief of the shipyard there.

And after Messina, he should go to Bivona to see what don Aurelio Spanò, marquis of Puntamezza, was up to, since it was almost certain the gentleman was lining his pockets with tax proceeds, as the people of Bivona were claiming. Lastly he said that subsequent to all the expropriations being conducted of the money and properties of corrupt officials, the revenues might perhaps make it possible to reduce taxes a little.

Donna Eleonora showed great interest in this argument and asked the Chief Treasurer to explain. He replied that, indeed, money was pouring into state coffers by the bushel.

The marquesa then ordered that the arrest and conviction of don Simone and his friends should be brought to the public's knowledge by the town criers, who must cover every street in the capital.

She then announced that she would explain everything she had in mind to do at the next Council on Friday.

And she adjourned the session.

She'd invited the princess of Stabia and don Serafino to lunch and didn't want to be late. She wanted to talk to them at length about the plans she had in mind.

* * *

When the great door of the palace was closed and locked every evening, it was the custom that, aside from the guards outside, who stood ten steps away from one another all along the walls, twelve elite soldiers, who changed from week to week, would remain inside, under the command of Lieutenant Ramírez, who was always there.

Of these twelve soldiers, three stood guard in front of the

Viceroy's private apparentment, another outside the door, a second halfway down the corridor, and a third at the top of the stairs leading to the floor below.

Normally, after an hour or so, seeing that nothing ever happened inside the palace, the guard at the top of the stairs would lie down on the floor and go to sleep.

The other two would likewise fall asleep, but on their feet, like horses, with their backs against the wall.

That week the three soldiers assigned to guard the apartment were called Osorio, who was outside the door, Vanasco, who was the one halfway down the corridor, and Martínez, who was at the top of the stairs.

That night, while in a deep sleep, aided by the semidarkness created by the fact that the only torch lighting the hallway was far away, Osorio was suddenly awakened by something he didn't at first understand.

Was it a human voice or an animal?

He pricked up his ears and soon became convinced that he was hearing the voice of a man moaning in pain.

"Ahhh! Ahhh! Ahhh!" said the voice.

What was a man doing inside the private apartment where there were only supposed to be women—that is, donna Eleonora and her four chambermaids?

Hearing the desperate laments continue, he went over to Vanasco, who was asleep, and woke him up.

"Come with me," he said.

"What is it?"

"I want you to hear something."

Vanasco followed him and heard the moaning.

It was possible that someone had entered the apartment through a different door. But that door led directly into the room where don Angel's catafalque rested.

The two men ran to Martínez and woke him up.

"Have you seen anyone pass this way?"

"Anyone . . . ?" Martínez repeated, still half asleep.

"Yes, a man."

"No," said Martínez, who, in a sleep as deep as his, wouldn't have seen even a whole army pass.

All three went to listen to see whether the voice was still moaning.

It was.

"I'll go and call the lieutenant," Osorio said, worried. "You two don't move from here."

Lieutenant Ramírez arrived on the run, a burning torch in his hand. He too heard the cries, which grew more and more frightening.

Now all of them were scared.

"Go and wake up the Chief of Ceremonies and get him to bring the key to the private apartment."

The other key was in the possession of Estrella, the chief chambermaid.

The Chief of Ceremonies arrived in his nightshirt and opened the door. They all went into the antechamber.

It was immediately clear that the cries were coming from the room in which don Angel's corpse was lying.

Everyone's hair stood on end, and they all started trembling. They were scared out of their wits.

"Who has the key to that room?" asked Ramírez.

"Donna Eleonora."

"Isn't there any other door?"

"There is, there's a second door that gives onto the landing. But it's always been locked," said the Chief of Ceremonies.

"And who has the key?"

"I wouldn't know."

Then the lieutenant went up to the locked door and asked: "Who are you?"

There was no answer. The moaning, however, became more terrifying.

Voice now quavering a little, the lieutenant asked:

"Do you need help?"

"Yesssssssss!" replied a cavernous voice that sounded as if it came from the bowels of the earth.

The torch fell from the terrified lieutenant's hand and went out, plunging them all into darkness.

At which point they crashed into one another and fled into the hall, where they remained, out of breath and clinging to each other.

At that moment the groans stopped.

They all pricked up their ears but no longer heard anything.

The following morning the Chief of Ceremonies and Lieutenant Ramírez respectfully asked donna Eleonora if they could have the key to the room where the dead body lay.

"Last night we heard a man moaning in there," said the Chief of Ceremonies.

"He was asking for help," added the lieutenant.

"*Estáis seguros?*"

"Absolutely."

"*Voy con vosotros.*"

Inside the room, everything was in perfect order. The great candles in the candlesticks were still lit. Lieutenant Ramírez went and checked the other door.

It seemed not to have been opened for years.

The Chief of Ceremonies and lieutenant felt upset. But the look donna Eleonora gave them made them feel even more upset.

That same morning Osorio, the soldier, who had a thing going with the palace chambermaid whose job it was to buy provisions in town, told her about the terrible fright he'd had. And she, who was quite a gossip, told it to everyone at the market.

The following night nothing happened. All hell broke loose, however, on the night between Thursday and Friday.

At half past midnight the two soldiers on guard on the first floor, whose names were del Rojo and Sánchez, were leaning against each other, asleep, when they were awakened by a sudden blast of cold air.

Since it was a nasty night of wind and rain, apparently a gust had opened a window somewhere. A second later, owing perhaps to another gust, the only wall torch went out.

The two guards immediately became worried, knowing what had happened three nights before.

They didn't manage in time to go and relight the torch before a bonechilling, lost-soul lament paralyzed them.

Then, by the light of a thunderbolt, they saw a frightful thing.

A ghost, with both arms raised, was approaching them menacingly, emitting that groan, which one couldn't hear without being scared to death.

"*Una aparición!*" shouted del Rojo.

"*Un fantasma!*" yelled Sánchez.

And both took to their heels, shouting wildly and so loudly that they woke up half the palace.

The only open route ahead of them was the staircase. They took it and ran past Martínez, who was in a haze of sleep.

"*Una aparición!*"

"*Un fantasma!*"

Martínez started running behind them, adding his voice to the screams.

When the three soldiers came to Vanasco, who was the bravest of the lot, he let them pass but remained steadfast at his post, sabre unsheathed, waiting for the ghost to arrive.

Osorio came running up and planted himself beside him.

And the white ghost appeared at the far end of the corridor. But it was not alone.

Behind him was another ghost.

Two ghosts was too much to bear. Both Vanasco and Osorio likewise turned tail and started running behind the other three, to the end of the corridor.

"*Dos apariciones!*"

"*Dos fantasmas!*"

And thus they were not in a position to notice that something odd had happened. Which was that the first ghost, hearing a loud moan behind him, had turned and, seeing the second ghost, had fainted and fallen to the floor.

This was because the first ghost wasn't really a ghost, but the Chief of Ceremonies, who'd been woken up by all the yelling and got out of bed in his white nightshirt and the tasseled white cap he normally slept in.

Stepping over the ghost on the floor, the second ghost kept advancing, still moaning and groaning like a lost soul.

The soldiers, by this point spooked out of their wits, had nowhere to run, the only remaining escape route being the window.

But at that moment Sánchez remembered that just under the window was a little terrace. Small and narrow, but a terrace just the same.

Without thinking twice, he opened the window and threw himself below. The other four followed behind him, still shouting:

"*Dos apariciones!*"

"*Dos fantasmas!*"

All the yelling, meanwhile, had woken up donna Eleonora. She got up out of bed and went out of her apartment and into the corridor, where she ran into the lieutenant, who was bearing up a trembling, saucer-eyed Chief of Cermonies, arms around his shoulders, as the official blubbered:

"A gh . . . ghost! I s-saw a gh . . . ghost!"

Half an hour later it was learned that Sanchez, in jumping

out the window, had leapt too far out and instead of landing on the little terrace had crashed some twenty yards farther below, at the base of the palace walls, and died instantly.

Donna Eleonora decided that it would be quite inappropriate to hold the Council session the following morning. She would tell the Councillors what she had to say to them at the Tuesday session.

And since it wasn't possible to talk to the Chief of Ceremonies just then, she sent for the assistant chief and told him to inform the Councillors, first thing in the morning, that the session had been postponed.

By this point she longer felt sleepy, and so she went into the study to read the letters that had been coming in, since by now people were writing to her from all over Sicily.

The episode of the ghost left her indifferent, but she planned to discuss it with Lieutenant Ramírez in the morning. She was convinced it was a nasty prank among soldiers that, unfortunately, had ended badly.

As the first light of dawn was coming in through the window, however, Estrella appeared and told her that there was a priest in the anteroom who needed urgently to speak with her. She got up and went to meet him.

She'd never seen this priest before. He was rather young, had wild eyes, and was decked out in a stole and holding a holy-water bucket and aspergillum. He didn't greet her, but only stared fixedly at her.

"*Quién es Usted?*"

"I am Don Scipione Mezzatesta, the new palace chaplain. Don Asciolla was reassigned."

"*Qué quiere?*"

"The key to the room where your husband's mortal remains lie."

"*Por qué?*"

"I believe it is my duty to undertake the immediate burial of the deceased. The ghost who appeared this evening is clearly your husband, who is wandering about bewailing that he has not yet been granted a Christian burial."

Black flames flashed in donna Eleonora's eyes.

"*Fuera de aquí!*"

"I shall have to notify his excellency the Bishop that—"

"*Fuera de aquí!*"

The priest turned his back and went out.

That same morning the bishop sent word to all the local parish priests to inform their congregants that at noon the following day, Saturday, he wanted everyone gathered together in the Cathedral because he planned to celebrate a Mass for the troubled soul of don Angel, after which he would deliver a special sermon. And then on Sunday morning there would be a solemn funeral procession that would leave from the Cathedral and march to the viceregal palace.

At midday on Saturday in the great church, there wasn't room left for so much as a needle. A great many people remained outside, not having been able to enter.

To ascend to his pulpit the bishop had to wend his way through the crowd, which overflowed onto the stairs leading up to it.

He knew that he had started a battle with donna Eleonora that could only end with the disappearance, in one way or another, of one of them. And he'd decided to speak without casting any anathemas, and to try to use only words that touched the heart.

He opened by declaring that all the gold in the world would never persuade him not to say the words he was about to say. In addition, these words, if taken the wrong way, could lead to grave charges against him, namely that of having rebelled against the representative of the power of our beloved sovereign, the King of Spain.

So why, then, was he speaking?

Not in obeisance to a higher order, but only to give voice his own conscience as a pastor who had to find ways to make his entire flock follow the holy precepts. And among these holy precepts, there was one in particular that must not be transgressed: the injunction to bury the dead.

"My little brothers and sisters, my sons and daughters, has it ever once crossed your minds not to give a Christian burial to one of your loved ones? To your father? To your mother? It never has, I am sure of it. And one who does not want to bury the dead, what kind of person is that? A man or a beast? A beast, you will say. But, be careful, my little brothers and sisters: there are people who have the appearance of human beings and the feelings of beasts. And these people can only be either possessed by the demon or incarnations of the devil himself. And right here, in Palermo—and my heart weeps to say it—there is a woman who, if she is not the demon herself, belongs to him. Do you know of whom I speak?"

"Yes!" said a thousand or so voices.

"This woman," the bishop resumed, "refuses to bury her husband, and keeps his dead body in her house. Why is she doing this? Is it perhaps—and the mere thought of it makes me tremble—because she needs that body for some of her devilish black magic? And the other night, as you all know, the deceased's poor soul started wandering from room to room groaning and pleading for help. Because his wife will not grant him the peace that is his due."

"The woman is cursed!" cried a very shrill, almost hysterical voice.

"Cursed! Cursed!" hundreds of voices repeated in unison.

"And do you want to know something else?" the bishop continued. "Yesterday morning she dared throw out the priest who wanted to bless the deceased just to grant him a little peace!"

There was a long murmur of shock and disapproval.

At this point all it took was for one woman to fall to the ground, foaming at the mouth, for dozens of others to follow suit. Some knelt and beat their chests with their hands, some tore at their hair, some writhed on the floor, eyes rolling back into their heads . . .

With all the power in his lungs, the bishop announced that the solemn procession would leave from the Cathedral at nine the following morning, and then he stepped down from the pulpit.

He was pleased with his effort.

And since in a short while the content of the bishop's sermon came to be known at the palace, Lieutenant Ramírez, weighing his options, requested that the number of soldiers guarding the building be tripled and was granted his request.

The bishop, too, for his part, held a long meeting with Mezzatesta and four other trusted priests, during which they worked out all the details of the next day's procession and of what would follow the procession.

In the early afternoon, a worried don Serafino raced to donna Eleonora to warn her that there was a great deal of uneasiness in the city over the question of her unburied huband and the supposed ghost in the palace. And as he knew nothing of what had transpired, since he hadn't been to the palace since the previous Tuesday, he was filled in on everything. Afterwards, he sat for a few minutes in silence, then asked donna Eleonora for the key to the room with the catafalque. The marquesa gave it to him without any questions.

The court physician went and spoke with the Chief of Ceremonies.

"I wanted to ask you about what happened the other night."

"When I saw the ghost?"

"I'm not interested in the ghost."

"Then what do you want to know?"

"Where the cries were coming from."

"Definitely from the room with the viceroy's casket."

"Is it true that the lieutenant asked the person crying if he needed any help?"

"Of course. And the person said yes. I heard him with my own ears. And the voice was coming right from there."

"I'm told that there's a second door there."

"That's true."

"Who has the key to it?"

"I don't know."

He thanked the Chief of Ceremonies, went and opened the door to the mortuary chamber, went in, and closed it behind him.

Don Serafino didn't believe in ghosts. The four candlesticks gave off sufficient light. He looked around.

And he noticed that in the wall on the right-hand side of the room there was a large recess, the sides of which were carved into trompe-l'oeil columns supporting an arch. Surely in the past the room must have been a chapel.

He approached the door at the back, which was large and old, and studied it long and hard, examining the lock in particular.

He was starting to form an opinion, but he needed to ask a few questions.

CHAPTER TWELVE
Processions, Clashes, Talking Corpses, Ghosts, and Other Things

Don Serafino went down to the chapel on the ground floor. The door was ajar. He pushed it open and went in. There wasn't a soul inside. He slipped into the sacristy, but there wasn't anyone there, either.

He was on his way out, intending to come back later, when he heard some sounds from the little door that led from the sacristy to the apartment reserved for the chapel priest.

He went in there and found Don Asciolla packing some clothes into a bundle. Don Serafino had known him for years and admired him. He'd always seemed to him a man who minded his own business, discreet and concerned with doing his job as a priest and nothing more. They exchanged a warm greeting.

"I hear you've been replaced," don Serafino began.

"Indeed. After twenty years here. I've seen a few viceroys come and go! And never once . . . but, never mind."

"I'm sorry. But why the replacement?"

Patre Asciolla threw up his hands.

"His excellency the bishop didn't deign to give me an explanation. And I've no choice but to obey. The Lord's will be done. It was only by chance you found me here. I'd just come to get my belongings."

"And where's the new chaplain?"

"At the bishopric with the bishop. He and his excellency are hand-in-glove, if you know what I mean. They're busy preparing the funeral procession. But my question is: What's wrong with this poor Christian widow wanting to bury her husband in Spain? I performed the service for the dead on him myself, and gave my blessing. Therefore, from the point of view of the Church, everything's in order."

"Do you know when your replacement will be back?"

"I wouldn't know. All the same, I don't think he'll be back here before tomorrow afternoon."

"Tell me something. Since you've been here at the palace for twenty years, it's something you ought to know. That room in the private apartement where don Angel's casket is now, what was it used for before?"

"It was the chapel. Then, a year before I got here, this chapel here, which is larger, was completed. All the stuff that was in the other one was brought here, and the old chapel became just another room."

"How many doors did the old chapel have?"

"There were always two. The viceroy and his family would come in through the door to the private apartment, while everyone else, including the chaplain, would use the second door, the one on the landing, which has been locked ever since."

"Do you know who has the key to this second door?"

"Of course. It's right here."

He went over to a piece of furniture, the upper part of which featured a great many little drawers, opened one, took out a large key tied with string to which was a attached a piece of paper with the words: *old chapel key.*

"Could I borrow it? I'll bring it right back."

"All right, but be quick, because I'm about to leave."

He went upstairs to the second floor, stopped outside the door, inserted the key, turned it, but it wouldn't move. The lock was stuck. He tried again to turn it, harder this time, but there was nothing doing.

There were two possibilities: either the lock was too rusted to function, or that was not the right key.

Or it might also be a case of . . .

He pulled his shirt out his breeches, took one tail, rolled it up tight and, standing on tiptoe, stuck it into the keyhole, pushing it as far inside as he could.

When he pulled it back out, it was all stained.

Not with rust, but with oil.

He went back downstairs and returned the key to the priest. Then he asked him the logical questions.

"What is the name of the priest who has taken your place here?"

"Don Scipione Mezzatesta."

"Does he know the story of the old chapel?"

"Yes, he said his excellency the bishop told him about it. In fact, when he arrived he asked me where the key to it was."

"And did he try it?"

"No, sir. Why should he try it? He only wanted to see it."

Don Serafino left the chapel feeling satisfied.

He was absolutely certain he'd guessed right. And he wanted to go at once and tell donna Eleonora. Which he did. He also explained to her what he had in mind to do, and she gave him free rein.

* * *

Some two thousand people were gathered outside the Cathedral, while inside there were another thousand or so. The parish priests had given it their all, threatening their flocks with excommunication, illness, and divine retribution if they didn't attend. And every one of those present—between shouts, imprecations, insults, blasphemies and curses hurled at the viceroy, on top of the cries, wails, laments, Ave Marias, and Pater Nosters—made enough noise for three.

Some thirty-odd priests, conveniently placed both inside the great church and outside, were handing out crucifixes of varying size and hundreds of papier-mâché death's-heads with the words *Bury me!* written on the forehead, which were to be borne aloft on spikes.

The nuns and friars of all the convents and monasteries of Palermo opened the procession by reciting the Rosary.

Following behind them were a hundred priests singing the prayer for the souls of the dead.

Just behind them came a baldachin borne by four priests, as people threw flowers and roses down on it from the windows and balconies above. Under the baldachin, in golden vestments, the bishop walked very slowly, holding before him, with both hands raised, the sunbeamed golden pyx with the Most Holy Sacrament inside.

Behind him a queue of another hundred priests recited the litanies of the service for the dead.

Then three thousand shouting people, men and women, waved crucifixes and death's-heads in the air, spurred continuously on by some thirty-odd priests mixed in with their number.

"Louder!"

"Haven't you got any air in your lungs?"

"Hold your skulls and crosses high!"

"Haven't you got any strength in your arms?"

When the procession reached the great square in front of the palace, everyone could not help but notice the triple cordon of armed soldiers protecting it, and so the nuns and friars at the head of the cortege stopped a short distance away. All they could do was raise their voices, so that the Rosary could be heard all the way inside the palace.

Then, a short while later, the crowd opened up fanwise so that those carrying crucifixes and death's-heads could come up to the front row and join together in a chorus of many voices— a chorus they'd practiced when they were all gathered inside the cathedral.

A first group chanted:

Get out of Palermo, woman of ill-fame!
Get out alone, the same way you came!

While a second continued:

Bury the dead in holy land,
unhappy woman, woman damned!

Then the two groups came together:

Woman, just bury the dead,
then off to hell you must head!

Then, after repeating the chorus three times, they stepped back and made room for the bishop, who came forward slowly, alone, without the baldachin but still holding the Holy Sacrament.

All present fell to their knees. The bishop recited a prayer that seemed never to end, but when he was done he made the sign of the cross three times in the air with the pyx of the Sacrament.

The procession now over, the bishop, after giving the people his benediction, went back to the cathedral, accompanied only by the four priests carrying the baldachin.

But the event didn't end there.

All the nuns, friars, priests, and the three thousand people remained in the square, where four makeshift altars had been set up. Masses for the salvation of the soul of don Angel were to be recited without interruption until sunset.

The best part came when, that afternoon, half of Palermo left their homes to go and see what was happening outside the palace, and there soon wasn't room for so much as a salted sardine. A few scuffles even broke out among the new arrivals, because there were some who sided with the bishop and others who instead claimed that donna Eleonora could have her husband buried whenever and wherever she bloody well pleased.

As soon as the sun set and the Masses ended, the bishop came back to the square to commence the second part of the great protest against the failure to bury the viceroy, which consisted of a nocturnal novena, by torchlight, which would continue without interruption until five o'clock the following morning.

Shortly before midnight, Father Scipione Mezzatesta, who had been egging the faithful on all the while, went up to the bishop, said something inaudible to him, took his leave, and went into the palace through a secondary door, which was the one nearest the chapel.

Despite the great pandemonium outside, all was calm inside.

The only new development was that the soldiers standing guard on the first and second floors had been relieved earlier than expected by other soldiers that Lieutenant Ramírez had personally hand-picked.

After midnight, however, they too became sleepy and dozed off.

And this was what enabled the ghost, who materialized on the ground floor, to climb the stairs unseen and reach an open first-floor window. He appeared in the aperture and began shaking his arms in the air like someone desperately calling for help.

And since there was a torch right under that window, a number of people spotted him and started shouting:

"The ghost!"

And the cry spread, repeated from mouth to mouth:

"The ghost!"

Finally the bishop cried out:

"Do you see him? It's the restless soul of don Angel! It's that diabolical woman who has reduced him to this state!"

Everyone fell to their knees.

Meanwhile the ghost had withdrawn and gone up to the second floor, stopping outside the door to the former chapel.

He opened it noiselessly, went inside, immediately smelled the odor of death in the room—despite the fact that the court physician and the coffin-maker had done a good job—but hadn't had time to close the door behind him before a hair-raising, sepulchral voice called out from the casket:

"Who are you to disturb my eternal sleep?"

"Ahhhh!" cried the ghost, scared to death, promptly turning tail and running out of the room.

The soldier on guard, who, as ordered, had only been pretending to be asleep, got up at once and tried to nab him, but the ghost eluded him and started running down the stairs. At the fourth stair, however, he stumbled and rolled all the way down to the landing below.

Standing up, he got rid of the sheet covering him and dashed, limping, towards the secondary door, pursued by the soldiers and don Serafino, who for the past hour had been waiting for him, hiding behind don Angel's casket, so he could play that wicked joke on him.

Father Scipione Mezzatesta realized that if he was able to reach the bishop he might manage to avoid arrest. The moment he came out into the square, still running, he started shouting:

"Help! I'm Father Mezzatesta and they're trying to arrest me! Help!"

At this point the soldiers caught up with him, grabbed him, lifted him into the air and carried him inside. There, don Serafino and Lieutenant Ramirez were waiting for him.

"That was clever of you," don Serafino said to him. "You took the key from its drawer and replaced it with another similar one, even adding the tag to identify it. But it went badly for you anyway."

"I want to talk to the Grand Captain of Justice," said Father Scipione, suddenly calm.

"Why?"

"I want to tell him that everything I did was on the orders of his excellency the bishop. I hope he will take that into account."

"I hereby inform you that you are under arrest," Ramírez concluded, just to make things clear.

Outside, meanwhile, the recitation of the novenas had broken off.

Between the ghost's apparition and news of the arrest of Patre Mezzatesta, a kind of fuse had been lit and burned slowly through the great mass of people until they exploded in fury and rage.

Quivering with an irresistible desire to let off steam, they all waited for the word from the bishop, who meanwhile was standing aside, surrounded by a handful of priests.

Turro Mendoza was quite worried because, knowing Father Mezzatesta well, he knew he could not be trusted. Sooner or later the man would confess to everything and reveal that the idea of the ghost was not his own. And he would have no qualms about naming him as the sole person responsible for the whole tragic farce. For that reason he had to do something to get him released as soon as possible.

He didn't know that Patre Mezzatesta had already maneuvered to finagle a lesser sentence, and that any attempt to keep him from talking was by now useless.

The bishop told the priests to work up the faithful's exasperation and hysteria as much as possible and then have them attack the soldiers guarding the palace.

"But those guys'll kill us all at their leisure!" said one of the priests. "We're unarmed!"

"Our weapon is our faith!" the bishop replied harshly.

"All right, but with our faith all we can do is die, we can't very well hit a soldier over the head with it!" the same priest replied.

"Then order everyone to arm themselves with stones, sticks, iron bars, whatever they can find that can cause injury. Break the branches off the trees in the square and turn them into cudgels!"

And if we're lucky, somebody'll get killed! the bishop thought to himself.

That way the faithful's fury would become unstoppable, and it was anyone's guess how it would all end.

As soon as the captain commanding the triple array of soldiers outside, whose name was Villasevaglios, saw that the people were arming themselves with sticks and stones, he realized that things were taking a very bad turn. They were no longer dealing with shouts and prayers but with beatings, and ferocious ones. And so he sent a lieutenant to talk to donna Eleonora to find out how he should proceed.

He received very precise orders. The marquesa wanted, at all costs, for there to be no dead or wounded amongst the people, should they decide to storm the palace. The soldiers could indeed use their sabres, but only the flat side, never the tip or the cutting edge.

All at once a crowd of about five hundred hurled themselves at the soldiers, shouting angrily:

"Free Father Mezzatesta!"

"Sacrilege!"

"Devil out of Palermo!"

The first attack was repelled. Five or six soldiers were taken inside with their heads cracked open from clubs or thrown stones.

About half an hour went by before a second attack was launched. Don Valentino Puglia, who had been a soldier before becoming a priest and was one of the bishop's trusted men, took command and better organized the nearly three thousand people, enraged out of their wits, who no longer demanded just the burial of don Angel and the liberation of Patre Mezzatesta, but also the expulsion of donna Eleonora from Palermo.

Meanwhile hundreds of pitchforks, mattocks, and spades were taken from nearby houses and passed out among the men that seemed the most hot-headed.

The second assault was more violent than the first. The soldiers barely managed to push back the attackers, but only after a long clash that at moments was so unbridled that the soldiers lost another ten or so men to variously serious degrees of injury.

It was clear that if the people launched a third assault, the soldiers would have to yield if they couldn't use their weapons. Captain Villasevaglios, who had asked for emergency reinforcements, was biting his nails with each passing moment, worried that they might not get there in time.

Meanwhile it was becoming more and more unlikely that that there wouldn't be any wounded among the attackers. One couldn't rule out that some soldier, finding himself in a hopeless situation, might use his sabre not as a club but as a proper sabre.

At this point don Serafino, seeing how dangerous the situation had become, tried to persuade donna Eleonora to leave the palace and go and stay temporarily either at the soldiers' compound or on one of the warships docked in the port. But she wouldn't listen to reason, and there was no way to make her change her mind.

While Don Valentino Puglia was giving the order to attack again, this time with two thousand people, all equipped with lethal objects, something happened that nobody in the world would ever have expected.

Some three hundred men, all considerably young and strong, suddenly and very quickly poured into the square. They were shouting as one, with all the air they had in their lungs:

Long live donna Eleonora!
Donna Eleonora is ours!

They were members of the guild of stevedores of the port, and they immediately started punching and kicking the faithful. And with each punch, one of the crowd fell, unconscious.

Then some five hundred members of other guilds came running in, after they were woken up in the middle of the night to come to donna Eleonora's aid.

And then Captain Villasevaglios ordered a counterattack.

In this way the faithful found themselves threatened from the front and the rear at the same time.

The first to run away was the bishop.

Once he was gone, there was a mad stampede of retreat.

Half an hour later, there was hardly anyone left in the square, because the men from the guilds had all gone home to try and recover a little of the sleep they'd lost, and the soldiers had fallen back to their positions around the walls of the palace.

Early in the afternoon of the following day, don Filippo Arcadipane requested an audience with donna Eleonora, to inform her that he would be going as soon as he could to officially interrogate Father Scipione Mezzatesta.

And since the priest had confessed the night before to the court physician and Lieutenant Ramírez that the whole episode of the fake ghost had been cooked up and ordered by the bishop to stir up trouble for her, it was possible that during the interrogation he might not only repeat his confession but add that it had likewise been the bishop behind an even more serious act—that is, having incited the people to rise up against the person who not only represented absolute power but was the alter ego of His Majesty the King.

In the past, all those who had done the same had been arrested and condemned to death.

As a result, with the law on his side, he, as Grand Captain of Justice, would, as a first, unavoidable measure, have to send the bishop immediately to jail.

But this would surely trigger a serious reaction in the city, where the situation merely appeared to have calmed down, but was actually smouldering under the ashes.

He therefore wanted to know how he should proceed.

Donna Eleonora's answer was to wait until the afternoon of the following day, Tuesday, to interrogate Patre Mezzatesta, because the Holy Royal Council was scheduled to meet that morning. This was a decision that had to be carefully considered and discussed by everyone.

In the mid-afternoon, Patre Mezzatesta, who until that moment had remained relatively tranquil in the bodyguards' cell, suddenly started yelling that he wanted a priest, because he wanted to confess and take Communion early the next morning.

Lieutenant Ramírez, when informed of this by a soldier, couldn't decide whether or not to accept the detainee's request.

He talked about it with the Chief of Ceremonies, who went and told donna Eleonora about it.

She granted the request, but advised the soldiers not to take their eyes off him for even one second.

CHAPTER THIRTEEN
Donna Eleonora and Her Laws

An hour later, Don Valentino Puglia presented himself to the palace guard. He'd been chosen personally by the bishop, and had received detailed secret instructions on how to behave with the detainee.

The bishop was certain that Mezzatesta would ask him how much he was willing to pay for his silence. And he wasn't mistaken.

Don Puglia's meeting with Patre Mezzatesta lasted more than two hours, and to the soldiers standing guard outside the door, all the angry shouting sounded more like a squabble than a confession.

When he came out, Don Puglia told the guard commander that he would be back the following morning at six, and that he would celebrate Mass in the chapel. Therefore the detainee had to be brought there shortly after six, since he wanted to take Communion.

Don Puglia hurried to tell the bishop what Patre Mezzatesta wanted in exchange for refusing to confirm to the Captain of Justice the confession he'd made to don Serafino and Lieutenant Ramírez. He was ready to swear that he'd said what he'd said to them in a moment of anger, that the idea to create the fake ghost had been his own, and that the bishop not only had nothing to do with it, but didn't even know about it—but only on the condition that . . .

"So, in conclusion," said the bishop, "Mezzatesta wants me to make certain they give him the minimum sentence, demands five thousand scudi at once, and then, once he's served his time, he wants to be appointed priest of the Sacro Cori parish, which is the richest in town, the one that receives the largest bequests. Is that correct?"

"Quite," said Don Puglia.

"Then tell him that I cannot accept two of his three requests. He must content himself with the five thousand scudi. Tell it to him before you give him Communion."

"And what if he doesn't accept?"

The bishop bowed his head pensively. Then raised it again. And before speaking, he looked Don Puglia long and hard in the eye. The other understood in full the content of that silent exchange.

"If he doesn't accept, give him Communion."

Don Puglia arrived at the chapel at six the following morning. The priest got ready for Mass, put the only host he'd brought with him into the chalice, and closed the tabernacle.

A short while later, Patre Mezzatesta came in with a soldier on either side of him.

"Last night I sinned in my thoughts and need to confess," he said to Don Puglia.

"Very well," said the priest, going and sitting down in the confessional.

Patre Mezzatesta went in the other side and knelt down.

Don Puglia leaned out of the confessional and asked the soldiers to stand farther away, at the back of the chapel.

Soon the soldiers began to hear the two men's angry voices. They started to approach but did not arrive in time, because Patre Mezzatesta had stood up in a flurry and gone over and started kicking Don Puglia, who responded with a powerful punch that sent Patre Mezzatesta's head crashing against the wooden corner of the confessional.

A moment later Patre Mezzatesta, foaming at the mouth, fell to the ground, unconscious.

When he recovered, he seemed a different man. He asked Don Puglia to forgive him, confessed again, prayed while listening to the Mass, stood up to receive the consecrated host, then returned to his place.

When it was over he let himself be led back to his cell without any fuss, merely saying to the soldiers that he had a terrible headache from the blow.

Half an hour later a guard looked into the spyhole and found him lying on the floor. He unlocked the door, went in, and touched him, but there was nothing more to be done. Father Scipione Mezzatesta was dead.

The soldiers who'd witnessed the scene in the chapel told don Serafino that they were certain that he'd died from the blow to the head.

But a blow to the head—and don Serafino knew this perfectly well because he was a very good doctor—would not cause a generalized bodily swelling and turn the victim's lips blue.

Those were clear signs of poisoning.

And the poison could only have been given to him through Communion, by means of the consecrated host.

And even he, who believed in nothing, felt profoundly troubled by this.

Donna Eleonora, on the other hand, remained cold as ice when he went into the study to tell her the conclusion he had reached. Don Serafino couldn't accept this.

"I'm sorry, my lady, perhaps I didn't make myself clear enough. The bishop—"

Donna Eleonora raised a hand and silenced him.

"*Mi querido don Serafino,* I spent my entire youth in a convent and have known only one man, my husband. Nevertheless, I am able to recognize and judge men instinctively, and until

now I have never once been wrong.. From the very first
moment I have considered Turro Mendoza a man capable of
terribles atrocidades y igonominias. So this story of yours does
not surprise me."

"My lady, I do hope you realize that you have an enemy
who will not hesitate to—"

Donna Eleonora raised her hand again.

"I know. *Y estoy pensando en como defenderme.*"

"But you have no time to lose! Why hasn't the Grand
Visitor called him in for questioning yet?"

"Because that was *mi decisión.*"

"But why?"

"Because Turro Mendoza is *tan rico* that he can pay three
times what he illegally stole, without any difficulty. He would
be just *un poquito menos rico*, while losing none of his power,
pero con más sed de vendetta. No, ese hombre es una serpiente.
We must crush his head."

When she'd finished she looked don Serafino long in the
eye. The doctor suddenly felt weightless as a leaf and began to
float through the air.

"*No se preocupe por mí, amigo mío,*" said donna Eleonora in
her angelic voice.

"I can't help it," don Serafino blurted out. "Because, you
see, I lo—"

Donna Eleonora's beautiful, slender, soft, tapered, rosy
forefinger went straight to his mouth and rested its tip on his
lips.

"*Silencio!*" she ordered him in a soft voice. "Don't make the
mistake of speaking. *Y ahora vaya, necesito prepararme para el
Holy Royal Council. Ah, por favor:* you must dine with me this
evening. And finally: could you meet with Don Asciolla and
tell him I would like to see him at four o'clock this afternoon?"

* * *

The Holy Royal Council began right on time. And for the duration of the session, only donna Eleonora spoke.

To open, she informed the Grand Captain of Justice of the sudden death of Patre Scipione Mezzatesta, adding that since the priest could no longer be questioned, this practically precluded all possibility of action against the bishop.

She didn't say a word about any of the events that had taken place on Sunday and the night that followed.

On the other hand, she said she had an important new law to propose, one which, if approved, would go into effect starting the very next day. Considering that both the Chief Treasurer and the Chief Administrator had informed her of a large increase in the revenues recently received or soon to be received into the royal treasury, especially after the seizures and expropriations of property belonging to former Councillors, she had decided to lift the tax imposed on wheat used for breadmaking.

If the proposed law were approved, it would mean that, starting the very next day, the price of bread in all of Sicily would fall by nearly half. The larger families and the many hundreds of paupers for whom alms did not suffice to buy bread would benefit the most. The *catapani*—that is, the guards who watched over the markets—would have to make sure that bakers were charging the reduced price.

Were the Councillors in agreement?

The Councillors were thrilled.

So donna Eleonora told the protonotary and secretary to write up the law immediately, which she would then sign so that by early the next morning the criers could make it known to all.

Immediately afterwards she declared that it was her firm intention to establish two shelters to harbor the women of Palermo who found themselves in abject conditions.

The first would be located in the former Conservatorio

dello Spedaletto, which used to house the infirm poor and had been closed three years earlier. It would now admit virgins in danger, to wit, "those young women who, constrained by poverty and bereft of parents, roam about the city at night and sleep in the public streets." Before being accepted at the Conservatorio, the girls would have to submit to an examination by the midwife Sidora Bonifacio, to establish whether they were still virgins and had received no offense in any other part of their bodies. But the Conservatory would also accept already fallen maidens, that is, those who had suffered an offense to a part of their bodies but against their will.

The second shelter, called the Conservatory of Reformed Magdalens, would be located in the former convent of the Daughters of the Madonna and would host streetwalkers or women thrown out of brothels for no longer being attractive to clients because of their advanced age, women who often died on the streets of hunger and hardship.

These two shelters would be a burden on the Kingdom's purse only by half, in that the other half would be paid for by twenty thousand scudi taken from the *aposiento*, the gift of twenty-five thousand scudi granted by Sicily to every new viceroy, since don Angel had never spent any of his own gratuity. For donna Eleonora's personal expenses, her monthly appanage would suffice.

The remaining five thousand scudi of the aposiento would be split into one hundred parts of fifty scudi each, and would go to constitute a fund that would dole out wedding dowries to one hundred girls who did in fact have a mother and a father but came from poor families. The donation would be called the "Royal Dowry."

The Councillors were taken aback. Never before had a viceroy renounced his lavish *aposiento*. And not only was she renouncing it, she was using it to fund a great work of charity.

Turro Mendoza says this woman is the devil—thought the bishop of Patti—*but if all devils are like her, I'm ready to burn in hell.*

These two shelters, donna Eleonora continued, like the Royal Dowry, would be placed under the command of the Judge of the Monarchy, who would see to the recruitment of the personnel and to the everyday administration, in addition to preparing the proclamation of the dowry for impoverished girls. Did the Councillors have any objections?

The Councillors had no objections.

Then, to conclude, donna Eleonora said she had some information to give the Councillors. She had received an appeal for clemency on the part of the marquis Simone Trecca, who had been condemned to death. He wanted the death penalty to be commuted to life imprisonment.

She had denied the appeal without hesitation, and had even advised the alcalde that the marquis should be the last to be put to death, after having to witness the execution of the two assassins who had acted under his orders.

She communicated this fact with her usual angelic voice, and with no particular inflections in her voice, although nobody present could look her in the eye, where the flames were burning blacker than ever.

The session was adjourned and the next Council convened for the following Friday.

Before exiting, donna Eleonora asked Don Benedetto Arosio, bishop of Patti, if he would come to her apartment at four o'clock that afternoon. The bishop consented.

The first question donna Eleonora asked Don Benedetto and Patre Asciolla was whether all the priests in Palermo had taken part in the procession against her. Don Benedetto replied that five priests had come to him to tell him that they'd declared themselves ill so they wouldn't have to attend. For his part, Patre Asciolla said he knew seven who had refused to obey the bishop's order.

"That makes twelve, like the Apostles," Don Benedetto commented.

Donna Eleonora then explained to them that they must speak to these priests, who were the only ones who could be counted on, and ask them to call to the attention to the representative of the Judge of the Monarchy all the young or old prostitutes they saw abandoned on the streets who survived by begging for alms. She wanted the two shelters to be up and running within a week at the most.

And it all must be done, of course, without Turro Mendoza knowing about it.

Shortly thereafter Don Benedetto asked permission to leave. Left alone with Patre Asciolla, donna Eleonora said to him:

"I want you to come back to your Chapel apartment, tonight."

"But the bishop . . . "

"At the moment, I don't think he would dare oppose your return as the palace chaplain."

"I'll do as you say."

"*Bueno*. One last thing: Do you know how many little boys there are in the Cathedral's choir of angelic voices?"

"Yes, there are twenty of them."

"*Y sabe si* in the last few days any boys were taken out of the choir?"

Patre Asciolla looked at her in shock.

"How did you find out?"

"So someone has indeed been removed ."

"Yes. Or so I was told at the bishopric."

"But taking away *un niño del coro no me parece un tema tan importante* for people to be talking about at the bishopric."

Patre Asciolla gave her a slightly embarrassed look.

"That's true. But this little kid—I'm sorry, this child, was the most beautiful of all and had the most gifted voice, and so—"

"*Sólo por esto?*"

Patre Asciolla became even more embarrassed.

"Speak."

"Forgive me, my lady, but I really do not at all like to repeat gossip and insinuations . . . "

"*Es una orden.*"

Patre Asciolla swallowed twice before opening his mouth.

"Apparently the little boy's father . . . had a violent argument with the bishop and Turro Mendoza, screaming, had him thrown out roughly by Don Puglia."

"Do you know *la razón* for this argument?"

"No."

But as he said "no" Patre Asciolla kept his eyes lowered. And donna Eleonora realized that that "no" was really a "yes," but that the priest, by his very nature, was incapable of malice.

"Do you know at least *quién es el padre?*"

Patre Asciolla hesitated a moment, but the replied.

"The boy is the son of Mariano Bonifati, and his name is Cenzino. Bonifati is the most important oil merchant in town, he's a benefactor of the Cathedral, and his wife is the leader of the devotees of the bishop."

"*Muchas gracias.* And I repeat: You must return to your apartment by this evening."

* * *

That evening, as the two of them were eating alone, donna Eleonora asked don Serafino whether he perchance knew a man named Mariano Bonifati.

"The oil merchant? Yes, I do."

"Are you *amigos?*"

"No, just casual acquaintances. But why—"

Donna Eleonora seemed not to have heard the question.

"Do you know anyone from the family? *Como la esposa*, a brother, a sister . . . "

"No. However . . . "

"However?"

"The doctor who takes care of the family is a disciple of mine. Antonio Virgadamo. Do you think he would be useful to you?"

"*Claro que sí.*"

"Tell me what you want of him and—"

"Later," said donna Eleonora, cutting him off.

But don Serafino went on.

"But I should warn you. If you want to know anything that concerns my disciple Virgadamo specifically as the doctor of the Bonifati family, there is no point in asking him. He won't tell you; he's a young man of unshakable professional integrity."

"*Entiendo*," said donna Eleonora.

And she changed the subject.

Later, in the study, don Serafino, anxious to be of use, brought the subject back up.

"Why did you ask me about Bonifati?"

Donna Eleonora shrugged.

"I beg you, please answer me."

"There is no point in talking about it anymore ."

"'Why?'

"Because, based on what you told me, I don't think you're in any position to help me."

Help her?

That changed everything.

"Please tell me what this is about," said don Serafino.

"If I say you are not the right person for this, you must believe me," donna Eleonora said brusquely.

Don Serafino knelt down and took a hem of her clothes in his hands.

"I beg you."

Donna Eleonora gave in.

"Get up, *por favor*, and sit down."

Don Serafino obeyed. The marquesa went over to the desk, grabbed a sheet of paper and sat down in front of him.

"This is a message to me that a stranger delivered at dawn *esta mañana* to the captain of the guard. It's not signed. It's written in Sicilian, and it took me some effort to understand it. Read it and then forget it."

She handed it to him. Don Serafino took it and read it.

Lemme tell you what that pig of a bishop did to a poor little boy of the Cathedral choir who's called Cinzino. He hurt him so bad his father had to get the doctor to give him some stitches.

How can that great big swine keep causing harm to little children? Please do something about it.

Reading this, don Serafino turned as pale as a corpse. He gave the note back to the marquesa, unable to say a word. He felt choked with indignation.

"*Qué lástima!*" said donna Eleonora. "If only I could get rid of Turro Mendoza . . . *para siempre* . . . "

"So it wasn't just gossip!" don Serafino muttered.

"*Parece que no.*"

"But how did you manage to find out the name of the boy's father?"

"I ask."

Whom? But he answered his own question before he'd even formed it in his mind. Patre Asciolla. That was why she'd sent for him. And if Patre Asciolla was helping her, should he step back?

"I beg your leave to go," he said, standing up suddenly.

"*Muy bien.* But you'll be back later?"

"Yes, if that's all right with you."

"I stay up waiting, *toda la noche, si es necesario.*"

"I'll come in through the secret little door."

"*Perfecto.* I tell Estrella to expect you."

* * *

Don Serafino returned two hours later.

"I talked to Virgadamo. And you know what? He was looking for me himself."

"Was it to talk about the boy?""

"Yes. He wanted my advice on the matter. He wanted to know whether or not he should denounce the bishop. Virgadamo maintains that such foul abuse exempts him from keeping professional secrecy. I said I agreed with him. And Virgadamo is convinced that it was the father who wrote you that letter. He didn't sign it because he was afraid the bishop would retaliate."

"What will you do?"

"Tomorrow I'll go to the Grand Captain of Justice and file a denunciation. Meanwhile I'll pay a call on Bonifati and try to persuade him to join in ."

"Do you think you can?"

"I don't know, but it's worth a try."

That morning, when Bishop Turro Mendoza heard the criers' drums and voices again, he got nervous.

The last time around, half the population of the city, upon hearing of the new law concerning the guilds, had immediately gone into raptures for donna Eleonora.

So what could the accursed woman have cooked up this time to get the men and women of the church, or those who until then had remained indifferent, to come over to her side?

Worried, he ordered Don Puglia to go down into the streets to listen to what people were saying and then report back to him.

The news that the price of bread had been halved was a heavy blow.

It would not be easy to convince churchgoing people that reducing the cost of bread by half was the work of the devil.

He certainly would no longer be able to count on assembling three thousand people. Maybe a couple of hundred, at best.

No, he had to change strategy, drop the business of donna Eleonora not wanting to bury her husband and come up with something completely different, something lethal. But he couldn't think of anything.

Doctor Virgadamo, as promised, requested an audience with the Grand Captain of Justice, submitting as well a note from the court physician asking don Filippo Arcadipane to receive him as soon as possible because he had something very serious to discuss with him.

And don Filippo, who was quite busy at that moment, did receive him, making him wait barely half an hour in the antechamber.

"How can I help you?"

"I'm here to denounce the grave abuse of a small boy of six, at the hands of—"

Don Filippo interrupted him.

"Are you his father?"

"No."

"Are you a member of the boy's family?"

"No."

The Grand Captain thought about this for a moment.

"Who is the boy's father?"

"Mariano Bonifati."

"The man who trades in oil?"

"Yes."

"Tell me in what capacity you are making this denunciation."

"I am the doctor who was summoned by the father to treat the lesions the boy sustained from the abuse."

"Do you have the father's authorization to come to me?"

"No."

"Why did you come?"

"Because I consider it my duty to—"

"And why hasn't the father considered it his duty?"

"Because he's afraid."

"I understand. So you're telling me indirectly that the person who abused the little boy is a powerful man?"

Virgadamo was an intelligent lad and understood how the Grand Captain's brain functioned. And so he limited himself to replying:

"Yes, he's a powerful man."

"Are you sure?"

"About what?"

"That it was this powerful man who abused the boy. I'll rephrase the question. Who told you that it was this powerful man who abused the boy?"

"The father."

"And did the boy confirm this?"

"In my presence he couldn't speak: he was crying."

"Let me ask you then: isn't it possible that the culprit might be the father, or another family member, and that the powerful man doesn't exist and was merely created to cast the blame outside the walls of the home?"

"I would rule that out in the firmest manner possible."

"On what basis?"

"Based on the sorrow and anger the father displayed as he told me what had happened. He was truly upset."

"That's not enough for me."

"What do you mean?"

"I mean I can't accept your denunciation. You can be the main witness for the prosecution, but the denunciation must, by law, be filed by a family member. And you must understand that in cases of this nature a strict adherence to the law is not only my duty, but also the path of prudence. I'm sorry."

Don Serafino returned to the palace disappointed and embittered.

"I was unable to persuade Bonifati. He's too afraid. I'm sure it was him who wrote the anonymous letter, because he wants to see the bishop imprisoned, but he has no plans to come out. He told me that a few hours after his altercation with the bishop over the violence done to his son, a priest showed up at his house, a certain Don Puglia, who threatened explicity to kill him if he filed a denunciation."

"*El médico su discípulo*, did he go and espeak to the Gran Capitano?" asked donna Eleonora.

"Yes, and he gave me a full report. Unfortunately the Grand Captain couldn't accept his denunciation."

"*Y por qué?*"

"Because it can only be made by a family member."

They both remained silent for a few moments.

Then donna Eleonora took the anonymous letter, read it, and set it back down on the desk.

"*Bonifati escribe que* there have been other similar cases," she said.

"People have been talking about it in town for quite some time," said don Serafino. "But until now it all remained gossip and rumor . . . there was nothing concrete."

"Please do me a favor. Go to the chapel, *y si Padre Asciolla está libre*, bring him back here."

Ten minutes later, Patre Asciolla was in front of the marquesa.

"*Padre*," donna Eleonora began bluntly, "I have proof that the bishop really did commit *ese esecrable acto* on the boy we spoke about."

Patre Asciolla turned pale.

"What a disgrace!" he muttered. "How shameful for the Church!"

His eyes filled with tears.

"Please listen. I will now ask you a question, and you must give me an answer."

"As you wish, my lady."

"Do you know whether, before this case, people talked about similar cases?"

"Yes."

"Have any other boys been taken out of the choir?"

"Yes."

"When was the last time?"

"Three months ago."

"Do you know the boy's name?"

"Yes."

"Tell me."

Patre Asciolla was now sweating.

"Carlino Giaraffa."

"Just a moment," don Serafino cut in. "Do you mean Stefano Giaraffa's youngest son?"

"Yes."

"Do you know him?" the marquesa asked don Serafino.

"Quite well."

"*Muchas gracias.* You can go now," donna Eleonora said to the priest.

As soon as Patre Asciolla went out, the marquesa asked the court physician if he could go at once and talk to Giaraffa. Don Serafino twisted up his mouth.

"There's a problem. Giaraffa, who used to be the administrator of the public property of the church of Palermo, resigned without any explanation and has moved with his family to Catania."

"Do you know *donde vive?*"

"In Catania? No. But I can ask his sister, who still lives here because she's married to—"

"Can you go there right now?"

Donna Eleonora had barely finished asking the question before don Serafino was already out the door.

Consolata Giaraffa, who was married to don Martino Giampileri, a respected notary in town, was quite grateful to don Serafino because the court physician, years before, had saved a daughter of hers from an illness about which nobody understood anything. She was a woman with an open heart who spoke her mind.

"I need to know where your brother Stefano is living in Catania. I have to go and see him."

Consolata became worried.

"Is something wrong?"

"No. I just want to talk to him," don Serafino replied, trying to minimize the matter.

But Consolata was not a woman who gave up easily.

"I know everything there is to know about by brother. Maybe you can spare yourself the journey and just talk to me."

Well, why not?

"Could you tell me why he resigned and left Palermo?"

"He no longer got along with Bishop Turro Mendoza."

"But before that, they got along?"

"Absolutely?"

"Before what?"

Consolata did not answer, but only went red in the face. It was clear the subject was a source of pain and anger.

"Let me help you," said don Serafino. "Before he took Carlino out of the choir?"

"So you already know all about it!" Consolata burst out. "That stinking rascal of a bishop grabbed Carlino one afternoon, took him into his study, and had his dirty way with him in there. That night the child started complaining and crying and told his mother everything. The following morning my brother went and denounced the bishop."

Don Serafino opened his eyes wide.

"Really?!"

"Yes, sir!"

"And to whom did he report this?"

"To the Grand Captain of Justice, the prince of Ficarazzi. Who promised he would discuss the matter with the Holy Royal Council."

"Do you know if they discussed it?"

"Of course they discussed it. It was during the session of May the twentieth. Then he called on my brother and told him that they needed more proof, and that he would take care of it himself."

"And how did it turn out?"

"What happened was that one day later, a priest by the name of Scipione Mezzatesta paid him a call and told him he might benefit from a change of scene. My brother threw him out. Three days later, as he was playing in the street in the early afternoon with three little friends, his eldest son, eleven years old, was nabbed by two men and forced into a carriage. He was gone until that evening. When he returned, he said that they'd taken him to a house in the country, beat him bloody with a stick, and then brought him back to Palermo at night-fall, telling him to tell his father that he'd better clear out within a week, or else. And so my brother went to Catania. But what's happened now? Is there something new?"

"Yes. And this time I'm hoping to nail Turro Mendoza once and for all."

"May the Lord help you."

Donna Eleonora wasted no time. She'd just finished dining with don Serafino when the secretary of the Council came in, handed her the book in which he wrote his reports of the sessions, and then left.

They found what they were looking for in the summary of the proceedings of the twentieth of May.

> *The Grand Captain of Justice, begging the pardon of His Excellency the Bishop Turro Mendoza for what his function obliges him to say, brings to the attention of their Excellencies the Councillors that a denunciation has been made by one Stefano Giaraffa against His Excellency the Bishop Turro Mendoza, who is alleged to have committed the foul deed upon the plaintiff's son, named Carlino, a boy of six and a half years.*

His Excellency the Bishop, upon hearing these words pronounced, humbly asked His Magnificent Excellency the Viceroy permission to absent himself for the duration of the session so that it could proceed without the hindrance of his presence.

H.E. the Bishop having been granted permission and having exited, the Grand Captain asked His Magnificent Excellency the Viceroy whether said question, concerning the highest representative of the Church in the Kingdom of Sicily, rather than be put to discussion by the entire Council, might not be more properly debated directly with the person of the Viceroy, he being the born Papal Legate and as such the sole person to whom His Excellency the Bishop owed obedience and submission, with no constraint obtaining thereto by the letter of the Law.

His Magnificent Excellency the Viceroy replied that, as His Majesty King Carlos had expressly recommended that any use he made of the Apostolic Legacy must be of the utmost discretion, and it was better that he make no use of it at all, and as the matter concerned a vexata quaestio *that could create discord between the Kingdom and the Papacy, it did not therefore seem to him expedient at that moment to exercise this prerogative of his.*

The Grand Captain of Justice then informed the Council that, given the gravity of the charge, he had without further delay taken steps to discover the truth.

And he had learned that fifteen days before the denunciation, the boy's father, Stefano Giaraffa, administrator of the public properties of the Church of Palermo, had been relieved of his duties by H.E. the Bishop for embezzlement and misappropriation of funds and had filed a denunciation against him—a denunciation which the Grand Captain had recovered amongst the papers of one of his officers. Two scribes who had worked with Giaraffa had also, moreover, declared under oath that, upon learning of his dismissal, Giaraffa had made obscure threats against the person of H.E. Turro Mendoza.

Given the aforementioned findings, the Grand Captain proposes that the Council not proceed with the denunciation and that a procedure for high calumny be insituted against said Giaraffa.

The Viceroy declared himself to be of the same opinion. As the rest of the Council, to a man.

Upon returning to the Hall of Council, and learning of the Council's conclusions, H.E. Turro Mendoza besought His Magnificence the Viceroy to suspend the charge of calumny against Giaraffa, that the populace might forget that act of infamy as soon as possible and not derive therefrom further grist for the mill of malicious gossip against his person, of which there was already too much in circulation.

His Magnificence the Viceroy granted the request.

"It seems clear," don Serafino commented, "that the Grand Captain and the bishop conspired before the meeting of the Council to put on a little act. Just as it's clear that the denunciation for misappropriations is false and conveniently backdated. And the two scribes were either bought or threatened."

Donna Eleonora, for her part, remained silent. And for so long that at a certain point don Serafino, summoning all his courage, ventured to ask her:

"What are you thinking, my lady?"

"*Estoy pensando que cuando Su Majestad el Rey* advised my husband not to use his powers as Papal Legate, *yo no estaba presente*, and therefore I can ignore this advice. There is nothing written down. What do you think?"

"Do you intend to avail yourself of it?!" don Serafino asked, alarmed.

"Does *esta situación* make you afraid?"

"A little, if you'll forgive my frankness."

"*Por qué?*"

"Because every time a viceroy has acted as born Papal Legate he's had the support of the King, but a good part of the Sicilian Church has rebelled."

"*Lo sé.* Only as a last resort," said the marquesa, "could I use my authority as Papal Legate to strip him of his powers. I could already have done so, because he stirred up *la población contra de mi, que represento la persona del Papa.*"

"Why didn't you do it?"

"Because he would still have been free to continue his horrible misdeeds *sobre los niños.* And I want to stop him. I want him to die in prison."

She fell silent again. Then she said:

"Tomorrow morning I shall order *el Gran Capitan de Justicia y el Juez de la Monarquía* to come to the palace at nine o'clock. I want you to come, too, even if you don't take part in the meeting. I feel safer if you're nearby. *Entretanto*, please go back to this woman, *ahora mismo,* and have her tell you where her husband lives in Catania. I want to see him. He must know that justice will be served."

Early the following morning, before don Serafino left the house, a very worried Doctor Virgadamo came to him.

"What's wrong?"

"I went to Mariano Bonifati's house to see how Cenzino was doing, but nobody was home. The door and windows were all shuttered, and the neighbors couldn't tell us anything. I found ten laborers outside the locked front door, not knowing what to do. They couldn't get inside to work, and they had no news from Bonifati."

Don Serafino broke into a cold sweat.

A terrible thought crossed his mind.

What if their disappearence was the work of the bishop? It

was quite possible he'd learned of his visit to try and convince Bonifati to make the denunciation, and to cover himself he'd nabbed Bonifati and his whole family.

"What can we do?" Virgadamo asked him.

"We can't do anything," the court physician replied through clenched teeth. "All we can do is hope we'll see them alive again."

What enraged him the most, and practically drove him out of his mind, was his feeling of powerlessness.

For this reason he got to the palace early, so he could tell donna Eleonora what Virgadamo had said to him. The marquesa made no comment. The skin tone of her face had suddenly turned wan.

Don Serafino's news was in fact the first thing she talked about with the Grand Captain of Justice, who begged donna Eleonora to delay the session and sent for Aurelio Torregrossa, who was the finest of his men, a lawman born and bred who knew Palermo and environs like the back of his hand. He assigned Torregrossa the task of searching at once for Mariano Bonifati and his family.

At last the door to the study was closed, and the Council session began.

The marquesa had time to utter three words, "I thank you . . . " before she was interrupted by some insistent knocking at the door.

"Come in!" said donna Eleonora, a bit miffed.

The door came open and Aurelio Torregrossa appeared.

He looked confused and uncertain.

"I beg your pardon, but I don't know how to—"

"Get to the point," said don Filippo.

"Early this morning two guards were attacked for no reason by a man armed with a club, and—"

"I don't understand why you're here wasting our time

telling us this story," an infuriated don Filippo interrrupted him, "when I myself ordered you to—"

"Please let me finish, I beg you. The man was arrested, but then started shouting that he wanted to speak with the court physician. They tried everything to shut him up, but it was no use. And so then he said he wanted to speak with you, my lord Grand Captain. He says it's a question of life and death. Knowing you were here, my men brought him here to the palace. I've had a look at him, and he does not seem mad."

"Did you tell you his name?"

"He doesn't want to say it unless you're present."

"Excuse me, my lady," said don Filippo, standing up. "I'm going to go and hear what—"

"No, wait," said donna Eleonora, who was, after all, a woman and therefore curious. "I want to hear too."

Torregrossa went out and then returned holding by the arm a middle-aged man with torn clothes, face swollen from punches, and a gashed eyebrow with blood pouring out of it.

He was apparently unable to speak and needed to recover his composure. Donna Eleonora sat him down and asked for some water to be brought to him.

"What is your name?" the Grand Captain asked him.

"Mariano Bonifati," the man replied.

The first person to recover from the general shock was donna Eleonora.

E *l protomedico está aquí*," she said in a comforting voice. "Would you like to speak *en su presencia?*"
"Yes."

They sent for don Serafino, whom donna Eleonora had sent into the next room. The moment he saw Bonifati his face broke into a smile.

"If I'm here, it's because of you," Bonifati said to the physician. "You called me a coward because I was afraid to denounce the bishop, and since that moment I haven't slept a wink. And so tonight I gathered my family together and took them somewhere safe. Then I attacked the two guards so that I would be arrested. I was worried that if I just came on my own to make the denunciation, the bishop's men might be watching the guards outside the palace. At any rate, the guards and me are even. I gave it to them and they gave it right back to me. And here I am, at your service."

Don Serafino looked at donna Eleonora, who signaled to him to proceed.

"Are you prepared to denounce Bishop Turro Mendoza, and to confirm this in court, for committing the foul deed against your son?" asked the physician.

"Yes."

The Grand Captain stood up and called Torregrossa.

"With the Viceroy's permission, go into the office with Signor Bonifati and take his denunciation. Then be sure to get Signor Bonfati some refreshment and lodge him in our office.

Given the dangerous situation he'll be in once he files the denunciation, I shall hold you personally responsible for any attempts to harm him and for anything that might happen to his family."

Donna Eleonora intervened.

"As far as his family is concerned, *tengo una idea mejor.* Signor Bonifati, tell Signor Torregrossa where they're hiding. They should be brought here, under a military escort. I want them to be lodged at the palace until the bishop is safely locked up."

The session lasted an hour. The Judge of the Monarchy was of the same opinion as donna Eleonora—that is, that they must not bring the Apostolic Legacy into play. The matter should be handled through ordinary procedures.

The person to make the accusation would therefore be the Grand Captain of Justice.

The Captain then said that in that case, they must take into consideration that such a foul deed called for the immediate arrest of the offender as soon as the authorities had a certain amount of evidence in hand.

For this they had the ultimate proof: the testimony of the doctor who had treated the boy.

Must they now proceed with the arrest?

Donna Eleonora replied that in her opinion it was better to wait until the second denunciation was made by Giaraffa. And since neither the Grand Captain nor the Judge of the Monarchy knew anything about the matter, she told them the whole story.

And they were all in agreement.

That same day, though quite late in the evening, Turro Mendoza received a visit from someone he really hadn't been expecting.

It was don Severino Lomascio, former Judge of the Monarchy.

Though he said nothing, the bishop was quite astonished to see him in such a shabby, neglected state, with his shirt in tatters. Only the foxlike eyes were the same as always.

"I thought you were still in jail," said the bishop.

"Don Esteban let me out the day before yesterday," said don Severino. "And I who once had my pick of houses, now that I'm out of jail I don't know where to go."

"Why do you say that?"

"Because don Esteban has sequestered my two palazzi in Palermo along with the castle of Roccalumera."

"And what about your family?"

"My wife took our two daughters and went to stay with her sister in Girgenti and doesn't ever want to see me again. Luckily an old servant of mine gave me a bed and a dish of soup."

The bishop got scared.

Want to bet that don Severino, reduced as he was to poverty, had come to ask him for money?

"Can I be of service to you in some way?" he asked cautiously.

He had no choice but to ask. To his relief don Severino shook his head "no."

"The reverse," said don Severino.

The bishop balked.

"What do you mean, 'the reverse'?"

"Don't you know? I mean the other way around."

"The other way around compared to what?"

"I mean that it's *I* who may be of service to *you* in some way. And you must believe me when I say so."

"I don't understand," said the bishop.

"Well, I'll explain. This evening, as I was leaving my servant's house, I ran into a scribe from the office of the Judge of the Monarchy, a fine gentleman for whom I had done a huge favor when he was in office and who has forever remained grateful to me. And this scribe, with the utmost secrecy, revealed something very important to me, something that concerns you directly, which you know nothing about and which constitutes a great danger to you. So I thought it was best if I went out of my way to come here and tell you."

"Then tell me."

Don Severino yawned, blew his nose, looked down at his shoetops, and did not answer.

"Well?" the bishop insisted.

"It's worth gold," said don Serafino.

"I'll be the one to determine whether it's worth gold, after you tell me what this is about," the bishop retorted.

"You'll pay before and after," said don Severino.

Before and after? What did that mean?

"You want half the money before and the other half after giving me the information?"

"No. I want to be paid first for the information, and then twice as much afterwards, for telling you how to get out of your pickle."

"Are you joking?"

"No."

"So how much is this information worth?"

Don Severino closed his eyes. Then he opened them and delivered the blow.

"Three thousand scudi, taking into account that we're friends."

Turro Mendoza gave a start in his chair.

"Have you gone insane?"

"Does that mean no?"

"Of course it means no."

"Then I'll be on my way," said don Severino, standing up and heading for the door.

But before going out, he stopped, turned round, and asked:

"Does the name Bonifati mean anything to you?"

"Come back here!" said the bishop.

He'd wanted to shout his command, but the voice that came out of his throat was that of a turkey-cock being strangled.

Don Severino, grinning, returned and sat down.

But the bishop already regretted not having been able to stay calm. He put on an expressionless face.

"They say so many things about me . . . " he said.

"This is written down."

"What do you mean?"

"I mean I want three thousand scudi in front of me first."

"You want to dispossess me."

"You'll still be better off than having no more possessions at all, like me."

"Let's make it two thousand."

"Well, if that's how it's going to be, I now want three thousand five hundred scudi. And that may go up to four thousand."

"All right, all right."

The bishop sat there a moment, thinking it over. Then he stood up.

"Wait for me here. This will take a while."

"I have all the patience in the world."

It was a good forty-five minutes before Turro Mendoza returned, followed by Don Puglia carrying three small sacks full to bursting and quite heavy. The priest set these down on the desk and then left, closing the door behind him.

Don Severino removed the string holding each bag shut, opened them up one by one, then closed them again.

"Prior to anything else, I would like to tell you something entirely for free. It's not true that I came directly here after running into my friend the scribe. I went to my ex-servant's house and gave him a note on which it is written that I've come here to talk to you about Bonifati. If I don't return this evening, he will give this note to the Grand Captain. Do we understand each other?"

The bishop became immediately convinced that don Severino was lying. He hadn't written anything, but was only trying to cover his rear. He pretended to believe it.

"Perfectly," he said. "Now speak."

"Bonifati has denounced you for butchering his son."

The bishop acted as if he was having a heart attack. He made as if to stand up, but then fell back down in the armchair, shaking his arms in the air as if trying to grab something that wasn't there.

"He denounced me?!"

"And that's not all. They have proof. You haven't been arrested yet because donna Eleonora wants Giaraffa—whose earlier denunciation of you for the same misdeed, as you'll recall, was rejected by our Council—to return to Palermo to re-submit it. At this point, with two proven denunciations, you're screwed once and for all."

Turro Mendoza sat there saucer-eyed, sweat dripping down his brow and panting heavily. His entire body was mildly trembling, as a string of spittle dangled from a corner of his mouth. He was unable to speak. He gestured with one hand for don Severino to wait a minute.

"I'm sorry, but I have no time to lose," said the other. "I'll be back in an hour or so."

He grabbed the sacks, put them inside a larger sack that he'd been carrying tied round his waist, wrapped his cloak around this, and went out. In the antechamer, Don Puglia, who was sitting behind a table covered with papers, looked at him and stood up.

"His Excellency told me to come with you."

"I think His Excellency may have changed his mind," don Severino said to him smiling, "At any rate I think he needs you here."

*

When don Severino returned without the sacks, he found the bishop as pale as a corpse, but clearheaded again.

"I have no time to lose," he began, sitting down.

"Me neither," said Turro Mendoza.

"Then let's get straight to the point. Have you meanwhile come up with any ideas of how to get out of this?"

"No."

"I've done a count."

"What kind of count?"

"A count of how many days you've got until they arrest you. You've got about six or seven. I know about these things."

"And so?"

"And so donna Eleonora must be stopped before these seven days are up, before the Grand Captain gives the order to imprison you."

"And how can we do that?"

"I know how. And it's your only way out. The best part is that you yourself know it too, but you can't see it."

"Then make me see it."

"First the gold."

"And what if your idea doesn't work?"

"It'll work, it'll work, I assure you. But the more time you waste, the worse it is for you."

"Listen, I'll tell you quite frankly: I haven't got six thousand scudi here in the house. I have less than that."

"How much have you got?"

"Five thousand."

"Then all right."

The bishop stood up with effort.

"I'll go and . . ."

"We'll do as I say," said don Severino. "Listen carefully. I'll go out first. When you come downstairs with Don Puglia carrying the five sacks, you'll find a carriage outside the front door, with me inside. Don Puglia will give me the sacks and go back and lock the front door. Then, after Don Puglia leaves, you will get into the carriage and I'll tell you everything. Agreed?"

"Agreed."

The first thing don Severino said to the bishop as soon as Don Puglia closed the front door to the house, was:

"Let me warn you that I'm armed. If you set some kind of trap for me, you're a dead man."

"I've set no trap," said Turro Mendoza. "Now tell me the way out."

"The way out has always been there, right under your nose. And instead of taking it at once, you started screwing things up, stirring up the populace, giving sermons at the Cathedral . . . making ghosts appear . . . They told me everything, when I was in jail. You've got her weakness right before your eyes, and you can't—"

"Quit bullshitting," the bishop cut him off. "What weakness?"

"She's a woman," said don Severino.

The bishop flew into a rage.

"Give me back those five thousand scudi!" he yelled. "You are a thief!"

"And you're a stupid shit!"

"And how is that going to help me, telling me she's a woman? What will that do for me?"

"It'll do everything for you."

"How?!" the bishop shouted in despair.

"How? You immediately send a letter to the Pope and ask him how is it possible that his Legate in Sicily is a woman?"

For a moment the bishop was breathless.

"Holy shit of Jesus! You're right!" he exclaimed after he'd recovered his strength.

Getting out of the carriage, he went and started knocking wildly at the door. Don Severino's coach and the five thousand scudi took off at high speed.

Don Severino did not know, as the carriage rolled along and he contentedly stroked the five little sacks at his feet, that he was carrying death along behind him.

Indeed Don Puglia, the moment he'd gone through the main door of the bishop's palace, had quickly run across the interior courtyard and come back outside through a small door at the back of the building. Then he'd turned the corner and, hunching over to keep the coachman from seeing him, he approached the carriage from behind and climbed aboard, remaining upright with his feet on the axle and his hands grip-ping the metal handles used by footmen on the carriages of the nobility.

Shortly after the carriage had entered the woods of La Favorita, Don Puglia decided to spring into action. It was an old carriage, and the canvas covering had grown slack. By slightly shifting the position of his right hand and touching ever so lightly, he could feel the bulge created in the canvas by don Severino's shoulders leaning against it from the inside.

He took out his dagger and, hanging tight onto the metal grip with his left hand, raised it in the air and brought it down with all his might in the middle of the bulge. The blade tore through the canvas, the clothing, the skin, and the flesh of don Severino. Don Puglia kept still and let a few minutes pass, and then he touched the canvas and felt that it was damp. With blood, naturally. Only then did he extract the weapon. Now came the most dangerous part. He didn't know whether the coachman was young or old, and he didn't know whether he'd been hired or was a friend of don Severino. He raised his right foot as far as he could and stuck the toes inside the handle where his hand had just been. He then pressed hard to see whether it would bear his weight. It would. In a flash he was on his belly on the roof of the carriage, dagger between his teeth. The darkness was very dense, and he couldn't see a thing. He slid forward, fearing that at any moment the poles supporting the canvas might break. Then he realized that the coachman's shoulders were just a short distance in front of him, less than an arm's length away. He slid forward a little more. At that moment the carriage entered a stretch of road along which the trees grew more sparse. The wan moonlight was enough for Don Puglia to spring like a snake. The coachman let go the reins and without a word flopped to one side and then fell to the ground. In one bound, Don Puglia took his place, grabbed the reins, and stopped the two horses.

He got down from the coach, walked back to where the coachman had fallen, recovered his dagger, returned to the carriage, opened the door, pulled out don Severino's lifeless body, throwing it to the ground, then climbed into the box, turned the horses around, and headed back for Palermo.

As soon as he'd returned to his palace, Turro Mendoza had raced into the library and had all the candelabra lit, ordering his servants to lay out on the table all papers and books having anything to do with the Apostolic Legacy—a phenomenon unique in all Christendom, which concentrated in a single person, the King of Sicily, and therefore the Viceroy who represented him, all civic as well as ecclesiastical power. This fine idea was the work of Pope Urban the second, who in 1098 had it passed into law with the bull, *Quia propter prudentiam tuam.* But then everyone forgot about it for centuries, or tried to forget, until, in the late 1400s, a certain Gian Luca Barberio dredged it back up. And this created a big row with the pope, who no longer wanted to recognize it. And so there were a great many disputes, squabbles, spats, tiffs, and vendettas between the kings of Spain and a variety of popes. Until, in

1605, one Cardinal Baronio machinated the conclusion that the famous bull had not been written by Pope Urban after all, but by the antipope Anacletus, and was therefore worth less than a counterfeit scudo. The kings of Spain replied that they didn't give a holy fig about Cardinal Baronio, but wanted only to know what the pope himself thought about the authorship of the bull. The pope answered saying he needed a little time to decide. But then decades and decades went by and the papal decision had never come.

The bishop set aside everything he'd read and began to reflect when he was interrupted by Don Puglia entering the room.

"All taken care of. I recovered the five sacks and put them back from where we'd taken them."

The bishop did not ask him how he'd managed to get them back, though he could easily imagine.

"What have you done with the carriage?"

"I set fire to it after taking it far away from here. And I set the horses free."

"Good. Now go and get a few hours' sleep, because you'll be leaving in the morning."

"Where am I going?"

"To Rome. You must deliver a letter from me to the pope. And you cannot take longer than three days. If you succeed, one of those five sacks is yours."

"Then I won't bother to get any sleep. I'll go straight to the port. I'll need to hire the fastest sailboat I can find. It'll cost you a lot, but your letter will be delivered in three days time."

It took the bishop more than three hours to write the letter.

But when he re-read it, he found it masterly. Every word was a nail in the coffin of donna Eleonora.

In case the pope had forgotten, the letter began with a brief history of the Apostolic Legacy in the Kingdom of Sicily and how this had always been a source of malaise on the island.

A malaise which, in the past few days, had worsened because of the trouble in which he, as bishop of Palermo and head of the Sicilian Church, had found himself when, upon the death of the viceroy, the man's wife had taken office in his place.

Which made her, therefore, the new, born, Papal Legate.

Now, who had the Pontifical Legates always been? Cardinals, bishops, monsignors—all people who had taken the Holy Orders.

Had it ever happened before that the Legate was a woman? Not only had it never happened, but such a thing was unthinkable.

How, then, could a bishop obey a female Legate? Would obedience not smack of heresy? This was the question tearing his soul apart.

And this was why he, Bishop Turro Mendoza, with filial devotion, was entreating His Holiness the Pope to intervene at once with the King of Spain to have the viceroy repatriated and all her acts of government and fiat nullified, both *sub jure proprio* and *sub jure legationis*.

Most importantly, failing to take measures to eliminate such a *monstrum* in timely fashion would further complicate any definitive resolution of the question of the Apostolic Legacy in Sicily.

* * *

By six o'clock that morning, Don Puglia was already aboard a ship sailing for Naples.

The bishop had taken care to explain to Don Puglia, in minute detail, how he should proceed once he got to the papal court, and he'd even given him the name of the right person to turn to, a cardinal quite close to the pope and a good and trusted friend of his. Don Puglia followed his advice closely.

And thus the letter from Turro Mendoza found its way into the hands of Pope Innocent XI, freshly ascended to the papal throne, very quickly—that is, three days and seven hours after it had been written.

On the afternoon of the thirtieth of September, as Don Puglia was headed back down to Naples to take ship again and return to Palermo, a letter from the Pope to King Carlos left Rome. In it, the pontiff requested the termination of the investiture of donna Eleonora di Mora beginning the following day, the first of October, as well as her immediate repatriation to Spain, for in no way could she remain in Sicily as Viceroy, in as much as being viceroy also meant being the born Legate of the Pope, and a born Legate of the Pope could never, in any way, nor for any reason in the world, be a woman.

In the letter he also requested, as a logical, inescapable consequence of the aforesaid, that all the acts of law that donna Eleonora had instituted both as viceroy and as Papal Legate, be declared null and void.

Otherwise, the letter concluded, the Holy Father's most holy patience, and his most holy prudence concerning the Apostolic

Legacy in Sicily, might just suddenly run out, in which case, the Holy Father, with his most holy cojones busted, would, yes, give his much-awaited answer, but it would surely not be favorable to the opinion earlier expressed by the Kings of Spain.

And so, to be practical about things, wouldn't it be better to remove at once the object in question and let things remain a while longer the way they were?

* * *

Meanwhile, Stefano Giaraffa couldn't believe he was actually racing from Catania to Palermo to denounce the bishop a second time. When he learned that he'd been denounced by the bishop and then sacked, he was dumbfounded. He asserted that he'd never been either denounced or fired, and that he'd had to leave his administrative post and flee to Catania because of the threats made against him by the bishop.

He reported to the Grand Captain that he, too, had had to summon a doctor, don Silvestro De Giovanni, for his son Carlino, but that the physician had refused to testify, since he was the doctor for the entire bishopric and would have lost his job. But certainly this doctor, seeing the storm clouds gathering, would sooner or later decide to do his duty. Even if it took giving him a hint of the chance he might himself end up in the slammer if he didn't tell the truth.

And thus they came to the most delicate issue of the entire affair: How to arrest the bishop?

It was the first time anything of the sort had happened, and they had to think things over long and carefully before acting.

Donna Eleonora, the Grand Captain, and the Judge of the Monarchy were all in agreement that the less brouhaha, the better.

It was pointless to hope that the bishop would show up at the palace of his own accord upon being summoned, just as it was pointless to hope he wouldn't put up fierce resistance if they went to arrest him with fifty men-at-arms.

The best idea came from donna Eleonora.

"Is there *un pasaje interior* between the cathedral and the bishop's palace?" she asked.

"Yes," replied don Filippo Arcadipane. "The bishop can go directly from his palace to the cathedral through a door in the sacristy."

"We must keep this door locked. Have two or more soldiers posted outside it. The bishop must remain isolated in his palace apartment, which will be watched *día y noche* to prevent him from trying to escape. The cathedral must remain open for worship, so that no one can accuse us of abusing our authority. You, don Filippo, must tell the bishop, *hoy mismo*, of the decision we have reached as a result of the charges against him.

"But what about when he has to appear in court?" asked the Judge of the Monarchy.

"We shall ask him if he wants to admit his guilt. *Si dirá que sí*, he must present himself in chains. *Si dirá que no*, we shall take him by force after he has been convicted, and only then."

Contrary to don Filippo's expectations, Turro Mendoza remained relatively calm upon hearing the news that he should consider himself under arrest, and that only out of respect for his person had donna Eleonora decided not to send him to jail. He answered by saying that this was a great trial the Lord was putting him through, and that he was confident he would get through it with the strength of his faith. Don Filippo then asked him for a list of no more than ten people who would be the only ones authorized to enter and leave the bishop's palace. Among these ten the bishop included the name of Don Puglia, his secretary, who, he explained, was out of Palermo at that moment but would be returning soon. He was someone who should be allowed to come and go at all hours of the day and night.

The enormous episcopal palace, between main doors, secondary doors, carriage gates and stable gates, not to mention little doors more or less hidden, counted no less than twelve entrances, which was why the armed soldiers placed on guard outside numbered in excess of twenty.

And that was not all. These soldiers would stop the people entering, asking them the purpose of their visit and who they were going to see. It took barely half a day before all of Palermo realized that something odd was happening to His Excellency the bishop.

The first night passed quietly.

In the early hours of the following day, Inquisitor don Camilo Rojas y Penalta requested an audience with donna Eleonora.

She'd seen him only once before, when don Camilo came to bow in obeisance to her, and she had immediately disliked him. Skinny as a skeleton, he wore an eye-patch around his death's head of a skull, covering his left eye, which had been gouged out by a prisoner who, having nearly lost his mind after hours and hours of torture, had pretended to faint and then attacked him.

Don Camilo always came off as a sort of starving, wild beast, because for many years now the Holy Office's fortunes had been in decline. They couldn't find a heretic anywhere for love or money, all the witches had disappeared, and they never got to burn anyone at the stake in the public square anymore. Where had all the lovely auto-da-fés gone? Nowadays one had to settle for torturing false witnesses, husbands with two wives, people who slandered others and told lies about them. All stuff that fell under the purview of normal secular justice as well, leading often to jurisdictional disputes between the two courts.

Donna Eleonora had been expecting this visit ever since she

had the bishop confined to his apartment, and she was well prepared.

"I'm told that His Excellency Bishop Turro Mendoza is being confined in his palace," don Camilo began. "And so I've come here to deplore the fact that the Holy Office was not duly informed, in timely fashion, of the accusations against him. According to the custom and the law, those who have never infringed—"

"Do you know what they are?" the marquesa interrupted him.

"The charges? No, and I would appreciate it if you—"

"He is accused of committing a foul act against two little boys who were in the Cathedral choir."

The Inquisitor looked stunned.

"Are you serious?!"

Donna Eleonora looked at him but did not deign to answer. Don Camilo brought a hand to his forehead.

"That seems quite unbelievable to me!"

Again the marquesa said nothing.

"Has he confessed?"

"He says that this is a trial that God has chosen to put him through."

Don Camilo ran his tongue over his lips.

"If he is guilty, which is yet to be determined, I know how to make him confess."

The sound of these words struck donna Eleonora like a punch in the stomach. She looked at don Camilo coldly, narrowing her eyes into little slits.

"How can you be so sure that a man isn't telling the truth—or better yet, the truth that you want him to say—simply to end the torture to which you are subjecting him?"

"If the man says the truth I want to hear, he will at any rate still be telling the truth, because I know what is true."

Donna Eleonora couldn't stand it any longer. She had to get this man out of her sight as quickly as possible.

"And now that you know what the bishop is accused of . . ."

"Now that I know, I think there's no doubt that the case falls under the jurisdiction of the Holy Office. It involves a crime committed by a bishop."

"I don't want to quibble with you," the marquesa said sharply.

"Please forgive me," don Camilo said promptly.

"Pray, take up the question with the Judge of the Monarchy," donna Eleonora continued. "He is more competent in such matters than I."

Don Camilo bowed and made as if to leave. Donna Eleonora carried on speaking.

"I should, however, like to underscore that, as the born Legate of the Pope, I would have the authority to judge the case of a crime committed by a bishop. But, at the moment, I've no wish to do so."

* * *

That afternoon, when don Gaetano Currò, the Judge of the Monarchy, spoke with donna Eleonora, he seemed quite worried.

"I discussed things at great length with don Camilo Rojas y Penalta. Unfortunately we have no arrows in our quiver," he said.

"So, is he right?"

"Unfortunately, yes. There's nothing in writing, mind you, but it is the custom that common crimes committed by men or women of the Church are the concern of the Holy Office. All the more so if they involve a bishop and head of the Church of Sicily. No, I'm afraid don Camilo will have to handle this. He cited seven cases of priests, including one monsignor, who were condemned for the foul deed by the Holy Office in the last three years."

"Did you verify this?"

"Of course. I read all the sentences handed out over the past three years."

"Also *las causas absolutorias?*"

"Yes, even the acquittals."

"Have there been cases where the Holy Office has acquitted priests of committing the foul deed because they found the accusations untrue?" asked donna Eleonora.

"Yes, two."

The marquesa thought about this for a moment. Then she asked:

"Do you know what kind of relationship Turro Mendoza and don Camillo have with each other?"

The Judge of the Monarchy's face darkened considerably.

"To call them fraternal would be an understatement."

He paused a moment and then continued.

"That's what worries me. If they weren't friends, it would make little difference whether Turro Mendoza was tried by us or by the Court of the Inquisition. But now you've got me wondering whether this isn't all a maneuver whose ultimate purpose is to absolve the bishop of the accusations."

"As long as I am here, that will never happen," donna Elenora said firmly.

Don Gaetano Currò looked down at his shoes. The black flame that sometimes lit up in that woman's eyes was unbearable.

"What can we do?" the marquesa asked after a pause.

"For the time being, I would like some proof of our suspicions," said don Gaetano.

"Proof?"

"Communicate the Holy Office's request to the bishop, and wait to see his reaction. The Inquisition is synonymous with torture and any normal person would pay in gold to submit to the justice of a royal court. If, however, he accepts without objection to be tried by the Tribunal of the Holy Office, it means he's putting his trust in his friendship with don Camilo and knows he'll get off scot-free."

Don Gaetano returned to the palace two hours later. He'd spoken with the bishop, who considered it quite fair that he should be judged by the Holy Office.

So there was no longer any doubt: don Camilo Rojas y Penalta would conclude that the accusations were untrue.

"And so?" said donna Eleonora.

"And so we have no choice but to proceed as if don Camilo had never made his request," said don Filippo.

"And what will we gain from that?"

"Time, my lady. We will gain precious time. Before don Camilo has a chance to renew his request more forcefully, in writing, we have to have already judged and sentenced the bishop. The whole thing has to be settled as quickly as possible."

* * *

In the meantime, it was a fine, sunny day in Spain as well as in Sicily, and two important things happened this day.

The first was that His Majesty the King of Spain had promptly received the Pope's letter. And read it. He immediately convened a meeting of his councillors.

They had a brief discussion, and three hours later an answer was ready to be sent out.

His Majesty had little trouble acknowledging the serious predicament in which the Holy Mother Church had found herself, having a Papal Legate undeniably of the female sex to contend with. And for this reason, however heavy the matter might weigh upon his heart, he was prepared to recall donna Eleonora di Mora, marquise of Castel de Roderigo, to Spain.

But only on one condition, from which he would not waver. *Sine qua non*, as the Ancient Romans used to say.

And that was that, given the fact that donna Eleonora had acted well *sub jure proprio*—that is, as far as concerned the Kingdom—and given the fact that she had never used her power as Papal Legate, His Majesty did not see any reason why he should nullify any acts of government or laws already instituted by her or debated before the last day of September. These were matters that concerned the Kingdom of Spain, not the Papacy. If His Majesty the King were to annul the acts of the Viceroy, it might be viewed as undue interference by the Church in the affairs of the Kingdom. What's done, dear Pope, cannot be undone, and there's no turning back.

If the pope accepted these conditions, fine. Otherwise, the viceroy would not be recalled.

It was his choice.

In the meantime, awaiting His Holiness' prompt reply, His Majesty the King humbly and filially bowed down in devotion.

* * *

The second important thing that happened was that Cocò Alletto, a man of sixty, woke up.

It was not, of course, such an unusual thing for someone, at morning's arrival, to wake up.

The fact, however, was that Cocò Alletto did not awaken from a good night's sleep, but from a drunken stupor so long even he didn't know how many days and nights it had lasted.

It had all begun when his ex-boss, don Severino Lomascio, marquis of Roccalumera and former Judge of the Monarchy, thrown in jail and stripped of all his properties, had shown up at the single room in which Cocò had been reduced to living.

Don Severino had asked him if he would be so kind to give him a bed, and Cocò had lent him his own.

And shared his soup with him.

Then, the next evening, don Severino had returned in a rather agitated state.

"The wheel of fortune may just have turned in my favor, Cocò!"

He'd written a long letter and entrusted it to Cocò, saying that if he didn't return that evening, he must deliver the letter at once to the Captain of Justice.

And along with the letter, he had put a handful of coins on the table.

"These are for your trouble."

And he'd left.

Never in his life had Cocò Aletto had that much money, not even in the days when he worked as a manservant at Palazzo Lomascio.

He decided that it was best to remain awake to see whether don Severino came home or not. He put the coins in his pouch, grabbed a jug, went out to the nearest tavern, had them fill it with wine, returned, and started drinking.

He'd hidden the letter under the pallet that served him as a bed.

When the morning light shone in, he realized that don Severino hadn't returned.

He decided to finish the jug of wine and go to the Captain of Justice. But then he suddenly fell asleep.

When he woke up again, he didn't know how much time had passed. Then he became convinced that don Severino had just gone out. And so he got up and went to have the jug refilled.

That morning, however, he realized that a lot of time must have passed. Luckily there was still some water in the basin. And so he washed himself and headed for the palazzo of the Grand Captain, which was a place he knew well because he used to deliver letters there every other day when don Severino was Judge.

In fact the clerk receiving letters as well as requests and denunciations recognized him.

And, repeating the words don Severino had said to him, Cocò handed him the letter.

Which, one hour later, was before the eyes of the Grand Captain of Justice.

It began as follows:

Most Illustrious don Filippo Arcadipane, this letter is from one who was once Judge of the Monarchy and sat on the Holy Royal Council but today is only Severino Lomascio, a wretch reduced to poverty and forced to resort to the basest expedients to survive.

Survive?

If you are reading these lines, it can only mean one thing: that I am dead. Murdered. You should therefore know that the person who gave the order to kill me—probably to his secretary, who I believe is called Puglia—is His Excellency, Bishop Turro Mendoza.

Let me explain, with no pity towards myself first and foremost, the reasons.

And here the letter went on to explain how, upon having learned by chance that the bishop was about to be put on trial for committing the foul deed upon two little boys of the choir, he quickly went to see His Excellency to ask him for three thousand scudi in exchange for the information, and another six for revealing to him how to get out of his predicament.

Begging the honorable Captain's pardon, he confessed that he did not think it advisable to tell him in a letter what the solution was. This would remain between him and the bishop.

He was quite certain that Turro Mendoza would accept the offer and pay in advance.

But he was equally certain that the bishop would do everything in his power to recover the money paid out, by using the services of his secretary, Don Puglia. And this was why he, don Severino, was in mortal danger.

In his opinion, the most dangerous moment would be when he left the bishop's palace in his carriage with the little sacks of coins. And he believed that were Don Puglia to follow him, the pursuit could only end in the woods of La Favorita, which he was forced to drive through to reach the place where he would take ship.

He concluded with the hope that the letter would never reach the hands of the Captain of Justice.

But if it did, he expressed the wish that it would help to send the bishop to jail.

Upon finishing the letter, don Filippo Arcadipane remained pensive.

Since the letter had reached him, it meant that don Severino had been murdered, and the bishop had recovered his money.

But the letter was utterly worthless. The bishop could easily defend himself by saying that don Severino had made it all up.

There was something, however, that might make a difference . . .

He sent for Aurelio Torregrossa.

"Have there been any corpses brought into the Misericordia in the last few days that were found along the carriage road that runs through La Favorita?"

"Yes, sir, one. Of a man who owned a carriage, which he would put up for hire and drove himself. His wife identified the body."

Don Filippo pricked up his ears.

"And has the carriage been found?"

"No, sir."

"Find out the exact place where the corpse was found. Then we'll go there together."

"To La Favorita?!"

"Why not? It's a beautiful day today, a walk in the open air will do us good."

L   ike the good detective he was, Torregrossa didn't take long at all to discover the spot where the coachman had fallen to the ground, already mortally wounded. A little farther ahead, he found a second large bloodstain mingled with dust.

"Here there was definitely a second injured person."

"Yes, I can see it," said don Filippo. "But where did he end up?"

He got no answer because Torregrossa had tensed all up like a pointer. He started walking into the woods.

"Where are you going?"

He got no answer this time, either. He just stood there on the road, not knowing what to do.

Then he heard Torregrossa's voice.

"Over here, sir!"

Once amidst the trees, he noticed that there was a footpath not visible from the road. He followed it and soon found himself behind Torregrossa.

"Look here, sir."

Half hidden amidst the clumps of wild grass was a sort of hut made of tree-boughs, mud, and wood. Sitting on the ground in front of it was a man, who was staring at them.

They approached. The man, who looked about forty and had a long beard, dishevelled hair, a naked, very hairy chest, and wild eyes, didn't move.

"I need to ask you a few questions," said don Filippo.

"And you can go and get buggered, both of you," said the man.

Torregrossa's kick broke two of his teeth, as well as his nose. The man closed his eyes and fainted.

Torregrossa, who always carried a chain on his person, chained the man's hands and bound his legs with some rope. They went into the hut.

Some men's clothing of apparently high quality, including a jacket with a gash in the back and a huge bloodstain, was hanging from a nail. On the ground were two boots of fine leather.

In one of the jacket's pockets they found a gold signet ring with the coat-of-arms of the marquisate of Roccalumera.

There was no doubt about it. The clothes had belonged to don Severino Lomascio. The man had stripped the corpse and taken its things.

They went back outside. The man's eyes were open again.

"Where did you put him?" asked Torregrossa, raising his foot to deal him another kick.

"Look in back," the man muttered.

They went behind the hut and immediately noticed some freshly turned earth.

"It's not deep," said Torregrossa, crouching down.

He started removing the dirt with his bare hands.

Before long a face began to emerge.

"It's the marquis of Roccalumera," said don Filippo Arcadipane.

Without wasting a minute, the Captain of Justice ran to tell the Judge of the Monarchy about the letter and the discovery of the corpse, then they both dashed over to the palace.

Donna Eleonora couldn't believe what she heard. She made an immediate decision.

"Since the main charge is now *doble homicidio,* the case no longer falls under the jurisdiction of the Holy Office, but becomes a matter for the Royal Court. The two *crimenes contra a los niños* now become the second charge, and must therefore be judged by that same Court. Please inform don Camilo."

"Straight away, my lady," said don Gaetano Currò.

"When can the trial begin?" asked the marquesa.

"Even tomorrow morning, as far as I'm concerned," said don Filippo.

"I'm ready, too," said don Gaetano.

"All right, then, *que sea para* tomorrow. I would like, however, for the bishop to be present for *la primera sesión*."

"Does that mean he must appear before the court tomorrow in chains?" asked don Filippo.

"Chains or no, *quiero que sea presente*. It's his right, after all. And his detention should go unnoticed."

And this, indeed, was the problem. Don Filippo Arcadipane scratched his head because he didn't know how to do this.

By the time he got back to his office, he'd reached the conclusion that the only solution was to discuss the matter with Torregrossa.

"Let me get this straight," said Torregrossa, after don Filippo had explained the problem to him. "So, at sunset, the bishop's palace will be evacuated, so that the only people sleeping there are the bishop and his secretary?"

"That's right."

"And the bishop sleeps in his own bedroom, with Puglia the secretary sleeping in the antechamber?"

"Yes."

"And the great front door will be locked at sunset by the soldiers who will stand guard the rest of the night?"

"Yes."

"Could you do me a favor and tell the soldiers to let four men with a cart through to deliver some wine?"

Don Filippo balked.

"Wine?"

"Leave it to me."

Fifteen minutes after the great door of the bishop's palace was closed, a cart pulled by a cadaverous horse pulled up outside. On the cart was one man holding the reins, and three other men who were clearly half drunk.

In the middle of the cart, held fast by ropes, was a huge barrel.

"We're bringing the wine," said the man with the reins.

The soldiers on guard, who'd been informed in advance, didn't say a word and opened the great door.

Before going inside, the man said:

"Please leave it open, because we'll be coming back out shortly with the empty barrel."

The cart went into the courtyard and vanished from the view of the guards.

Torregrossa, who was the man with the reins, stopped it outside the door to the bishop's private apartment.

"Come on, lads, let's unload the barrel."

They took it down from the cart and set it on the ground on one of its flat sides. Then Torregrossa climbed up onto the cart, bent down towards the barrel, and removed a metal hoop with both hands, whereupon the entire upper part could be lifted like a lid. It had taken three hours to have the thing prepared by a master carpenter and master blacksmith.

"Let's leave it like that and go upstairs," said Torregrossa.

The door was open. They climbed two flights of stairs on tiptoe, then came to another door, this one closed.

"This leads into the antechamber," Torregrossa informed the others in a soft voice.

He turned the knob and pushed, and the door opened. Stepping back with the other two, Torregrossa made a sign to Luzzo Luparello, who was a colossus, to go in first.

Luzzo threw the door open and immediately looked around, pretending to be confused.

Don Puglia, still dressed, was sitting on the bed that had been set up in the antechamber, busy reading a map by the light of a candlestick. He shot to his feet.

"Who are you?" he asked in alarm.

And he immediately reached down and pulled out the dagger he kept in a special sheath strapped to his leg.

"I'm so sorry!" Luzzo said in a raggedy voice, like one who'd been drinking a lot. "But I'm lost and can't find my way out of this stinking palace."

"Get out!" said don Puglia, drawing near.

Which was a big mistake.

Because immediately Luzzo's fist to the pit of his stomach, followed by a mighty kick to his cojones, laid him out on the floor, unable to open his mouth.

In the twinkling of an eye he was bound and gagged by three men who moved without making the slightest sound, and then tossed onto the bed.

"May I?" Torregrossa then called out, opening the door to the bishop's chamber and going in.

Turro Mendoza, who was sitting at his desk, writing, looked up and blanched.

Then he stood up and, emitting a long wail, fell to his knees.

"Excellency, look, you're making a mistake: I'm not God Almighty," said Torregrossa.

"Don't kill me, for pity's sake! I beg you! I'll give you all the money you want! Spare me!" the bishop implored, folding his hands in prayer and trembling all over.

"Wrong again, Excellency. We're just here to take you to jail. We'll leave it to the executioner to kill you. It's your choice: are you gonna come quietly or make trouble?"

The bishop, who had feared the worst, resigned himself.

"Tell me what you want me to do," he said.

"Nothing. Just come with us."

Two men carried Don Puglia away.

Luzzo helped the bishop to descend the stairs, supporting his shoulders, otherwise the prelate, his legs having turned to mush, was liable to fall and break his neck.

First they stuffed Don Puglia into the barrel, all bound and gagged as he was.

The problems arose when it came time to put His Excellency inside. His feet and legs went in all right, but his belly immediately plugged up the opening, preventing the rest of his body from entering.

With two of the men holding the bishop's arms in the air, Luzzo tried to stuff the rolls of belly-fat into his body, but the mass of lard simply shifted first to the left, then to the right, still preventing the body from going down into the barrel.

Then the third man, along with Torregrossa, intervened, pushing in from the sides in counterthrusts as Luzzo pushed from the center.

"One, two, three . . . Push!"

And thus, one barleycorn at a time, by dint of pushes, squishes, nudges, and curses, the belly went through.

Torregrossa then lowered the hoop, making it impossible to open the barrel from the inside, but now there was another snag.

Because the four of them were unable to lift the barrel with the two men inside, they had to resort to an elaborate song and dance. That is, unhitch the cart, lean the tilting vehicle on its shafts, roll the barrel up onto them and into the cart, fasten it with ropes, and then hitch it all back up to the horse.

At last the cart, with its four men and the barrel, could leave the episcopal palace.

Later, in the prison courtyard, to get the bishop and Don Puglia out, they had to break the barrel.

* * *

That same evening only two keys, both rather large, were found among the bishop's clothes, and he stubbornly refused to say what doors they were for.

And so the Grand Captain, together with Torregrossa and ten other men, went and searched Turro Mendoza's private apartment. But they found nothing of any importance.

They were about to leave in disappointment when Torregrossa noticed that the table in the dining room had been set for two, and the dishes with cold food hadn't been touched. Apparently the bishop and Don Puglia hadn't had time to eat before they were arrested.

But what drew Torregrossa's attention was a tiny little cask of wine all covered in dust, resting on the table atop a wooden support. Opening the spigot slightly, he put his hand underneath and brought it to his mouth. It tasted exquisite, like an old wine of very high quality. His Excellency treated himself well.

"The bishop must have his own cellar," he said to the Grand Captain.

"Let's go and have a look."

They went down to the ground floor. Right beside the main entrance was another door. They stuck one of the two keys in the lock. It was the right one. The door gave onto a long staircase leading down. At the bottom there was a second door, made of iron. It opened with the other key.

It was a large cellar. After searching everywhere for two hours, they found a large hole behind a barrel. Piled inside were ten small sacks full of gold scudi. Two were stained with blood.

* * *

Nobody in Palermo knew that the bishop was awaiting

trial. Because donna Eleonora, so as not to arouse suspicion, had ordered the guards outside the episcopal palace to carry on as though His Excellency were still inside, in his apartment.

But before the trial began, Turro Mendoza raised an important objection.

His secret intention was to gain time as he waited for an answer from the pope. And so he said to the Grand Captain of Justice that he, as head of the Church in Sicily, could not be judged by an ordinary court, but only by a court of similar rank to his own.

Donna Eleonora and the Judge of the Monarchy discussed the matter and came to the conclusion that it should be the entire Holy Royal Council to pass judgment on the bishop, a procedure never used before.

Thus the lone novelty of the occasion was that a chair was placed in the middle of the great hall for the defendant. Donna Eleonora refused to attend.

The Judge of the Monarchy was appointed to preside over the proceedings, while the prosecution's case would be argued by the Captain of Justice.

"The first crime with which you are charged is that of having ordered the killing of don Severino Lomascio, marquis of Roccalumera, and of his coachman, Annibale Schirò, a crime materially carried out by your secretary, Don Valentino Puglia."

From the very first words, the bishop was stunned and taken aback. He'd expected to be charged with the foul deed, not with double murder. How the hell had they found out?

He broke out in a cold sweat.

He'd just remembered that don Severino had warned him that he had covered himself by writing a letter to the Grand Captain, but he hadn't believed him.

And indeed:

"The charge," don Filippo Arcadipane continued, "is supported by a letter from don Severino, stating—"

"A letter means nothing!" the bishop interrupted him. "In reality, the marquis of Roccalumera came to me asking for money, and I refused. This is his revenge."

"In the letter," don Filippo resumed, "the marquis lucidly predicts that, in order to recover the six thousand scudi you gave him in exchange for some precious information, you would have him killed by Don Puglia in the woods of La Favorita."

"'Predicts'! . . . It's all just talk! You have nothing in your hands that could—"

"We have recovered the body of the marquis, who· was clearly stabbed in the back. We have an eyewitness to the murder, who afterwards stripped don Severino's corpse, and in his cellar we found two small, bloodstained sacks of gold pieces."

The bishop realized he was finished.

He opened his mouth to say something, but no matter how he tried, no sound came out.

"Finally, I must inform you that last night Don Valentino Puglia confessed to the two murders."

Don Filippo neglected to mention that at the jail they'd used a wee bit of boiling oil, letting it drip onto his naked flesh one drop at a time, to persuade him to talk.

And he would make sure not say anything about it to donna Eleonora, either.

"I don't believe it!" the bishop found the strength to shout.

"Please bring in Don Valentino Puglia," the Grand Captain ordered the two guards standing on either side of the door.

They went out and returned holding Don Puglia, who couldn't stand up, by both arms.

Great burn marks were visible on his naked chest.

"Forgive me," he said in a faint voice to the bishop, who covered his eyes with his hands and said nothing.

Don Puglia was taken back outside.

"Do you admit to having ordered the killing of don Severino Lomascio?"

"Yes," said the bishop. "But I knew nothing about the driver."

"Let us move on to the second charge, that of having committed the foul deed upon two young boys of the cathedral choir. Principal witnesses for the prosecution are the two doctors who treated the boys after you—"

"That's quite enough," Turro Mendoza. "Quite enough. I confess to having subjected those two children to my desires. And, if you really want to know, it's something that's been going on for years, except that no one has ever had the courage to denounce me. But, I'm telling you now, I won't answer any questions. So let's end this now."

And they ended it then, because there was absolutely nothing more to do, not even to call the witnesses.

It was probably the shortest trial in the history of trials.

The bishop was taken into a room to await sentencing, while the Councillors had the door of the great hall locked so that no one could listen.

That Don Puglia, as the material executor of the crime, had to be condemned to death, none of the Councillors had any doubt.

There was quite a debate, however, and a lively one, over Turro Mendoza's sentence: death or life imprisonment?

Don Filippo Arcadipane maintained that there was no difference between those who commissioned murder and those who executed, and therefore the death penalty should be applied to both. For his part, the Judge of the Monarchy agreed with don Filippo but reminded everyone that even a life sentence for a bishop would have serious repercussions for relations between Spain and the Papacy, so one could only imagine the mayhem that a death sentence might trigger.

They put the question to donna Eleonora.

At first she said that she absolutely did not want to interfere in any decisions of the special tribunal. But then, in the end, she decided to state her opinion.

"I believe the bishop must be formally *condenado a muerte*. But at the moment of pronouncing the sentence, *el tribunal* will request that the viceroy grant clemency to the *condenado* by commuting the sentence to life imprisonment. I, of course, will then willingly grant the court's request."

And so it was done.

Then, Don Benedetto Arosio, bishop of Patti, with the marquesa's permission, wrote to the pope explaining how they had arrived at the painful decision to jail the bishop of Palermo, and that they now needed to arrange for a replacement.

But he decided to take his time posting the letter, and would wait until the bishop had already been in jail for a good week.

Meanwhile, however, the pope, upon receiving the letter from the king of Spain, had weighed his options and come to the conclusion that it was much more crucial to have the viceroy recalled to Spain than to insist on annulling her acts of government.

And thus he wasted no time answering His Majesty, saying he was ready to accept the conditions the king had presented.

If he'd known in time about the arrest and conviction of Turro Mendoza, he would certainly have raised a ruckus, but the bishop of Patti's letter arrived too late for that.

* * *

At the dinner table the evening of Turro Mendoza's sentencing, don Serafino noticed that donna Eleonora was melancholy. Mysteriously, however, the light veil that seemed to have fallen over her eyes did not dim their splendor, but made them even more like a bottomless lake, enchanted and enchanting, in which the night sky's stars were reflected and sparkled like flickering lights.

The marquesa didn't feel much like talking, and don Serafino respected her silence—even though he would have given more than his life, his very soul, to have known the reason for that melancholy, and to make it disappear.

Then, out of the blue, she said:

"All those who offended *mi esposo* have paid for it. *Ahora don Angel puede reposar en paz*, for I have avenged him."

"You did not take revenge," don Serafino said firmly. "You only served justice. All the Councillors were corrupt, and you had them punished for their corruption. The offense made to the viceroy was merely the result of their profoundly corrupt actions and thoughts. You are not the sort of woman to take revenge. It is not in your nature. There is only justice in your nature."

Those words were like a gust of wind that bears the fog away. The veil over the marquesa's eyes vanished at once.

Donna Eleonora held out her hand, laid it on top of don Serafino's, and kept it there.

"*Gracias.* You understand me better than I do myself."

CHAPTER EIGHTEEN
An Ending neither Happy nor Sad

I t was an exhausting morning for donna Eleonora. Between inaugurations and receiving a special visit, she had a lot to do, all without pause.

The first inauguration involved the Conservatorio dello Spedaletto, which had been entirely renovated and now housed its own endangered virgins; the second was for the Conservatorio of Reformed Magdalens, which welcomed former prostitutes who, owing to illness or age, could no longer ply their trade.

The ceremonies were both very simple. The marquesa had decreed that there should be no pomp.

Welcoming her and the princess of Trabia, whom the marquesa had wanted beside her on these occasions, was don Gaetano Currò, the Judge of the Monarchy, brimming with pride over the tremendous job he'd managed to do in such a short time.

And he had every reason to be proud. They'd been able to rescue two hundred and fifty orphan girls off the streets, and more than two hundred aging prostitutes.

And now, thanks to donna Eleonora, they had only days of serenity and peace ahead of them.

Despite the fact that the orphan girls had begged her insistently to say a few words after the benediction given by the bishop of Patti, the marquesa didn't want to open her mouth.

She limited herself to hugging and kissing the youngest of the girls, who was only thirteen.

She did the same at the other refuge as well.

She hugged and kissed the oldest of the residents, but this time she whispered four words into her ear:

"Rest well, *hermana mía.*"

The third inauguration was for the Conservatorio di Santa Teresa, which followed the other two and was held by the nuns of the same convent. This was the refuge for the already fallen virgins—that is, those who didn't pass Sidora the midwife's test, but who had been violated against their will.

Later she received a visit from the hundred girls for whom the royal dowry had been designated.

At the end of this very long morning, the marquesa returned to the palace weary but happy.

* * *

That afternoon don Esteban de la Tierna, the Grand Visitor, came to pay a farewell visit. After Palermo, don Esteban had been dashing all over the island like a rocket, sending a great many dishonest people to jail, from the chief shipbuilder of Messina and the marquis Aurelio Spanò di Bivona, who was embezzling tax receipts, to the financial officer of Catania and the administrator of Calascibetta, a certain Trupiano. And he had confiscated a very great deal of money, homes, and lands that had been acquired illegally, and it all ended up in the royal coffers.

"It will be my great honor to inform His Majesty of your lofty merits," were don Esteban's last words to donna Eleonora.

And he exited walking backwards, like a roper, as a sign of respect, never turning his back to her.

* * *

That evening, as donna Eleonora and don Serafino were

dining together, the conversation turned to the Inquisitor, don Camilo, who had limited himself to writing a formal letter of protest against the conviction of the bishop, but said no more. Apparently he could think of no other arguments.

Don Serafino told the marquesa that for twenty-three years in the sixteenth century there had been an Inquisitor in Palermo, don Luis Rincón de Páramo, who was such a bloodthirsty fanatic that he wrote down the first and last names of all the hundreds of people he'd had killed. And he added that among all those imprisoned by Páramo there was one born rebel, a man opposed to power and men of power by nature, but who was also a poet, a true poet. His name was Antonio Veneziano.

"*Un poeta? Conoce algunas poesías suyas?*"

"All I can cite from memory are a few of his octaves."

"Recite at least one for me."

"The octaves are in Sicilian dialect. If you like, I'll translate it for you afterwards."

"Please recite it, *entretanto.*"

Don Serafino knew a good ten of them, but at that moment could only remember one. And he didn't need to ask himself why.

I was caught by the loveliness
of your most divine visage,
your ivory brow, your ebony tress,
your mouth two rows of pearls the image,
your eyes where Love and the Graces impress
love and grace on those who pay you homage.
Woman, you are of beauty the picture,
a miracle of God, art, and nature.

But don Serafino had changed one word.

He'd turned the tress Veneziano sang of from "golden" to "ebony."

And the amazing thing was that he'd done so without realizing it.

"Would you like me to translate it for you?" he asked.

"*La he entendido perfectamente*," said donna Eleonora.

* * *

The following day, which was a Friday, there was a session of the Holy Royal Council. And something out of the ordinary happened.

That is, as soon as donna Eleonora declared the session open, the Grand Captain of Justice asked permission to speak.

"I speak," he said, "on behalf of all the Councillors, who chose to assign me this pleasant task. We of the Council wish that it be put on the record that to a man we consider ourselves supremely honored to have been called upon to participate in the enlightened decisions of the viceroy, donna Eleonora di Mora, marquesa of Castel de Roderigo, and we declare ourselves likewise unanimously ready to follow her in any further decision she may wish to take, as we harbor unlimited faith in her extraordinary, generous, magnificent gifts for governance."

Donna Eleonora spoke right after the Grand Captain.

"I wish to thank you all for the trust you placed in me, now and in future. But what I want to say is that the 'enlightened decisions,' as you call them, which I have taken, are only the fruit of an elementary lesson I learned all the years I lived in a convent, which is that *Dios he creado el hombre a su imagen y semejanza*. Ever since, I have always made sure to respect *todos los hombres*—meaning those, naturally, who are worthy of the name—for in them the image of God is reflected. It follows, then, that if we do not help those who suffer, *a quien sufre la injusticia, a quien se muere de hambre*, if we do not help the weakest—and women are always the weakest—we commit not only a sin of omission, but also the much graver sin of blasphemy. That is all. *Y ahora*, if you don't mind, let us move on to the subjects for discussion."

The secretary stood up, opened his mouth, and then immediately shut it when the Chief of Ceremonies appeared in the doorway, holding a sealed envelope in his hand.

"I beg your pardon, but . . . "

"What is it?" said donna Eleonora.

"A courrier has just landed with an urgent message from His Majesty the King."

"I'll read it after—"

"Please excuse me," the Chief of Ceremonies insisted, "but the envelope says: 'To be read immediately upon delivery.'"

"Give it me."

The Chief of Ceremonies came forward and handed it to her.

"*Perdonen*," donna Eleonora said to the Councillors as she broke the royal seal.

She read it, blanched momentarily, then brought a hand to her brow as though she felt dizzy.

The Council held its collective breath.

Then she said:

"I shall read it in Italian. Forgive any mistakes."

She read it in her usual steady voice, without inflection, as though the matter didn't concern her.

It is with utmost regret and genuine displeasure that I must order you to return at once to Spain, and to step down, beginning the first day of October, from your functions as Viceroy.

Pending the appointment of your successor, the functions of Viceroy will be filled pro tempore by the Grand Captain of Justice.

Your repatriation, we are keen to insist, has nothing to do with your actions, which have, on the contrary, been quite wor-

thy in our eyes, but simply with the fact that since the Viceroy of Sicily, according to the Church of this Monarchy, is the Born Legate of Holiness the Pope, it is not possible for a woman to occupy this high office.

I have had to bow to this conclusion after receiving a pressing request from the Holy Father.

Nevertheless, all acts of government decided and passed by you while still in office, until the thirtieth of September, having been achieved with a full respect for the Law and fully within your rights as Vicecroy, shall remain in effect and cannot be abrogated, altered, questioned or mooted by your successor.

A tomblike silence ensued.

The Councillors looked dumbfounded in their armchairs.

The only person to retain her self-possession was donna Eleonora.

"*Obedezco*," she said, facing the king's vacant throne.

Then she rose, lightly descended the three stairs, airily extended her hand to the Grand Captain of Justice, and pointed her long, tapered index finger at the thronelet, saying:

"*Ahora vuestro puesto es este.*"

Don Filippo Arcadipane stood up, pale and disconsolate.

"I'll not dare take that place," he said firmly, "so long as you are here."

"Please arrange for me to sail on Sunday *con mis sirvientas.* I would also like the casket with my husband's mortal remains to travel with me."

"It shall be done," said the Grand Captain.

"Why are you in such a hurry to leave us?" asked the bishop of Patti.

His question quickly became a sort of chorus of supplication.

"Why? Why?"

Donna Eleonora didn't answer. Slowly, she looked every one of the Councillors in the eye, one at a time. Then she said. "*Gracias.*"

And she turned her back and went out of the hall, looking as if she was floating several inches above the ground.

The first to give free rein to his tears was don Filippo Arcadipane.

By lunchtime the whole city already knew that donna Eleonora was no longer viceroy, by decree of His Majesty, and that she would be leaving Sunday evening for Spain.

Little by little, street beggars began to gather in the square in front of the palace, people in rags, crippled and maimed, people missing a leg or an arm, the blind, the sick, the deformed at birth. Every one of them was holding a piece of bread they'd been able to buy because they could now afford it.

And they came to eat in silence, and in thanks, in front of donna Eleonora.

The marquesa, meanwhile, was discussing matters with the Grand Captain, who had come to remind her that there was a whole protocol that had to be followed, a ceremony in which the people bid their last farewell to every viceroy leaving the island, and which could not be avoided.

But donna Eleonora wouldn't hear of it.

"Since I've been an anomalous viceroy, let the anomaly continue, *hasta el final!*"

But don Filippo wouldn't give in.

"My lady, I understand your reasons. But it is my duty to inform you that such a gesture on your part might be misunderstood—interpreted, that is, as a refusal to meet with that part of the nobility and populace who, though they may not have always actively supported you, certainly never opposed you."

In the end, donna Eleonora let herself be persuaded.

And they determined that the ceremony would be held the

following morning, from nine to noon, in the great hall of Council.

Then she spent the entire afternoon beginning to pack. That evening, when it was time to eat, she waited a long time for don Serafino, but he was nowhere to be seen.

At a certain point, donna Eleonora started to get worried. What could have happened to him? Her concern grew so great that she lost what little appetite she'd had.

And she went to bed without eating.

Don Serafino, however, had been lying down in his room for hours.

Having learned from an acquaintance on the street that donna Eleonora had been recalled, he'd rushed to the palace, where he ran into don Filippo Arcadipane, who was on his way out. And he had his bitter confirmation.

He lacked the courage to go upstairs and meet with donna Eleonora.

He would have started crying like a little boy.

And so he went back home, weak in the knees, and threw himself onto his bed in despair.

At nine o'clock on Saturday morning, the square in front of the palace was mobbed with the seventy-two guilds of Palermo and the *patri onusti*. A delegation consisting of two consuls, two fathers, and the Magistrate of Commerce was the first to be received.

Between princes, dukes, marquis, counts and barons, the representatives of the nobility numbered about a hundred.

Then came the turn of the high royal functionaries. The protonotary, the secretary of the Holy Royal Council and . . .

Donna Eleonora really hadn't expected to see the court physician appear before her with the red eyes of one who's been crying his heart out.

As don Serafino was bending down to kiss her hand, she said to him softly:

"I shall expect you for supper *esta noche. Es mi última orden.*"

The marquesa's afternoon was spent entirely with the Grand Captain, the Judge of the Monarchy, and the secretary of the Council, seeing to the transmission of her orders to her eventual successor. Donna Eleonora's hand grew weary from signing her name so many hundreds of times.

When they had finished, it was already dark outside.

Returning to her apartment, she asked the chief chambermaid if don Serafino had arrived.

"Yes, he's in the sitting room."

"He'll forgive me if I'm a little late."

She wanted to undress, bathe, scent herself, and put on a clean but very simple dress, a household garment. In so doing, she wanted to show herself to don Serafino as she felt herself to be in reality: just another woman, and not the viceroy she had been.

Yet, without wanting to, she achieved the opposite result. If earlier she had been like a fruit covered in marvelous foliage, now, without leaves, the fullness, color, and perfection of the fruit was like an explosion of beauty.

"Shall we go to the table?" she asked, opening the door to the sitting room.

Upon seeing her, don Serafino was unable to stand up at first.

She spoke only at the beginning.

"Why didn't you come yesterday?"

"I didn't have the strength."

"I was worried."

"I beg you please to forgive me. I was also . . . "

"You were also?"

"I was afraid to inconvenience you. Surely you had a great many things to do . . . "

"Your presence has never been 'inconvenient.'"

And they didn't exchange another word. They even avoided looking at each other. Then, inevitably, they came to the end.

Donna Eleonora rose. Don Serafino did likewise, but with great effort.

Donna Eleonora closed her eyes, reopened them, and took one step towards him. Don Serafino did the same. They were very close to each other.

"We must say *adios*," said donna Eleonora.

Her voice was barely a breath.

And she closed her eyes again. And don Serafino saw a tear, just one, a pearl, fall from her left eye and roll ever so slowly down her cheek, stop for a moment before dropping off, and . . .

His right hand caught it in his open palm. He then squeezed it tight in his closed fist, wishing that tear could penetrate his flesh to the point of entering his very blood.

And that miracle may even have occurred, as don Serafino heard his own voice say:

"I'll come with you."

"*Cómo?*" said donna Eleonora, opening her eyes and looking at him in dismay.

"I'll come with you," don Serafino repeated in a firm tone.

"*Pero aquí tiene una madre, una hermana . . .* "

"They'll find a way to accept it. It would take me only a week, no more, to leave my affairs in order."

"*Pero en España . . .* "

"I'll work as a medical doctor, as I do here. When your husband fell ill, I became friends with don Juan de Torres, the physician sent by His Majesty, and we still write to each other from time to time . . . He'll help me out."

"*Le esperaré*," said donna Eleonora.

Her hand then hovered in the air, light as a butterfly, and came forward and caressed don Serafino's cheek.

"I can only promise you a dinner invitation *tres veces a la semana*," said the marquesa.

"That will suffice for me."

The Admiral of the Fleet had made a powerful warship available to the marquesa. The time of departure had been set for sundown, but the people of Palermo had started to gather and crowd the port in the early afternoon.

A thousand Spanish soldiers were arrayed along the road that led from the viceroy's palace to the port, and another five hundred were lined up on both sides of great wooden wharf below the ship, which was flying the flags of Spain and Sicily from its bulwark.

At three o'clock the casket with the viceroy's body was loaded onto a wheeled platform pulled by four horses, escorted by a platoon of lancers, and hoisted aboard the ship.

At five o'clock donna Eleonora arrived in a carriage, alone. The carriage with her four chambermaids followed behind.

The ship's captain welcomed her aboard and led her to the cabin normally reserved for the Admiral.

Then the city Senate, the Holy Royal Council, and other high dignitaries arrived.

Among the latter was the court physician, who seemed merely touched, and not even so much.

Donna Eleonora came out on deck.

Such a cry rose up from the crowd that the Grand Captain's words of official farewell became incomprehensible.

From where the populace stood, crammed together and piling on top of one another, came an unending stream of goodbyes, farewells, thanks, and blessings, accompanied by an endless waving of handkerchiefs, dishcloths, rags, and shirts.

Donna Eleonora waved her hand in reply.

Then the sailors began to raise the moorings.

All at once a great silence fell.

And amidst the silence, the voice of Peppi Gangitano, a poet of the streets and taverns, rose up strong, and sang the following:

To circle the earth in its entirety,
the moon takes twenty-eight days.
Women know this, as does the sea,
for with the moon they're always in phase.

Your reign lasted one lunar circuit,
tho' it turned the night bright as day;
your laws of goodness brought a surfeit,
and did some of our suffering allay.

And now that your effort is ended,
Lady Leonore, look into our heart,
and deep therein you'll find a splendid
little moon, yourself, reigning apart.

the creation of a Magistrate of Commerce bringing together the seventy-two guilds of Palermo.

As for the measures she took to assist women, it should be stated that she put the Conservatorio for Endangered Virgins and the refuge for old prostitutes back in running order, as both had been abandoned for lack of funds, whereas the so-called Royal Dowry and the Conservatorio for Reformed Magdalens were entirely of her own creation.

Also hers was the reduction of offspring required to receive the benefits set aside for "burdened fathers" (*patri onusti*).

Since I was narrating a novel, I took a good number of liberties, but I won't bother to enumerate them. But I will reveal two minor ones.

The first is that donna Eleonora could not have brandished the scarecrow of Royal Visitor don Francisco Peyró at the time, because Peyró was already dead by then. He remained a legend for having sent to prison one of the highest state functionaries, Harbormaster Federico Abbatellis, count of Cammarata, and with him the Grand Treasurer of the Realm, the Secretary, and two high prelates, for embezzlement . . . He was ultimately stabbed to death near Viterbo on his way back to Spain. On his deathbed, Federico Abbatellis confessed to having sent the assassin himself.

The second: after receiving the letter relieving her of her duties, donna Eleonora immediately handed the reins over to the Grand Captain of Justice but remained for a while in Palermo, to the point that Cardinal Portocarrero was unable to move into the viceregal palace right away because it was still occupied. So he took the trouble of sending a reverential message to donna Eleonora, in which he wrote that she could remain there for as long as she liked, because he had found temporary lodgings in the bishop's palace, which fortunately, at the time, had no occupant.

My endless thanks also go to Valentina Alferj, for her invaluable collaboration in revising the text.

A.C.

ABOUT THE AUTHOR

Andrea Camilleri is widely considered to be one of the greatest living Italian writers. His Montalbano crime series, each installment of which is a bestseller in Italy, is published in America by Penguin Random House. Several books in the series have been *New York Times* bestsellers. His literary honors include the Nino Martoglio International Book Award. Born in Sicily, Camilleri currently lives in Rome.

AUTHOR'S NOTE

All but one of the chronicles of the Spanish Viceroys of Sicily, when they come to the year 1677, write without fail that the Viceroy don Angel de Guzmán died in Palermo that year and was succeeded by Cardinal Luis Ferdinando de Portocarrero.

In reality, however, they all make inexplicably—or all too explicably—a grave error of omission.

What they do not say is that between the death of don Angel and the arrival of Cardinal Portocarrero, Sicily was governed by a woman, even if only for twenty-seven days.

As he was dying, don Angel had left a written testament stipulating that he wanted his own widow, doña Eleonora di Mora, to succeed him. The will was ambiguous, in the sense that it didn't specify whether his widow should be appointed Viceroy *pro tempore*—that is, pending the designation of a new viceroy—or should remain such for so long as it pleased His Majesty. Whatever the case, the final decision was inescapably up to the King.

It should be added that this wasn't the first time that a viceroy, on his deathbed, named a relative as his successor. In 1627, Viceroy Antonio Pimentel, marquis of Tavora, appointed his son, eliciting a reaction from Archbishop Doria of Palermo, who had aspired to the same post.

And likewise in 1677, the bishop of Palermo aspired to become viceroy.

However, the Holy Royal Council, which included the bishop of Palermo, had no choice but to submit to the deceased's last will and testament, and thus donna Eleonora became viceroy, the only woman in the world at the time to rise to so high a political and adminsitrative office.

* * *

I came across the subject when reading an important work by Francesco Paolo Castiglione, his *Dizionario delle figure, delle istituzioni e dei constumi della Sicilia storica* (Palermo, Sellerio, 2010).

The author, however, devotes only a few lines to the story of donna Eleonora, scattered in a few of the different entries that make up the volume.

A few rare references can also be found in the third volume of the *Storia cronologica dei Viceré*, by G. E. Di Blasi, published in 1975 by the Regione Siciliana. This work is the one exception I mentioned at the start of this note.

Di Blasi dwells briefly on the removal of donna Eleonora from office because of the simple fact of her being a woman and, as such, unable to assume the authority of the born Legate of the Pope, a title inseparable from that of Viceroy. The person who'd raised the question was the bishop of Palermo, who'd been excluded from the Holy Royal Council by Viceroy donna Eleonora and claimed that she persecuted him.

There wasn't much to go on, in other words, but it was enough to glean the image of an extraordinary woman who was able to earn a great deal of respect for what she did in her very brief period governing Sicily.

Hers were definitely the lowering of the price of bread and